AMIAYA ENTE

Presents

Window Shopper

a novel

by

Charles Threat

Written by Charles Threat for Amiaya Entertainment, LLC

Published by Amiaya Entertainment, LLC

Cover design by www.mariondesigns.com

Printed in the United States of America

Edited by Antoine "Inch" Thomas

ISBN: 978-0-9777544-6
[1. Urban — Fiction. 2. Drama — Fiction. 3. Niagara Falls –Fiction.]

Acknowledgements

First, I must thank my higher power, whom I choose to call God. Without him nothing is possible. Next I'd like to thank Tania and Inch for making this book possible and helping me to fulfill a dream. To James Mathis, aka Jimmy DaSaint, a friend and fellow author. Thanks for inspiring me to write. I may never have written a book if not for your encouragement.

To William "Horror Man" Cole. Another friend and unpublished author. I pray that you are next, man.

To Sam House and "Big" Irv Dillard. You two read every word that I wrote, while I was in here at FSL ELKTON. Your words of encouragement kept me writing.

To "Lil" Kenny Stoffer, keep on writing. For a man so young, I feel that you've got a lot of talent. One day I'll be reading one of your books. To all of the ladies in Niagara Falls, New York that have played a part in my life. Your lives helped to inspire this book. Thank you all!

And a special thanks to the most beautiful young lady in the world...Miss Nathania.

And finally, thanks to all of the men on this H-Unit here at FSL ELKTON.

Chapter One

The police siren wailed. It startled the two girls that were walking down the street. They prepared themselves to run. A second police car sped around the far corner, heading toward them. They were trapped.

Sheka, a short-haired, sexily built, black girl, quickly swallowed two plastic packets. Each packet contained one gram of crack. The packets scratched her throat as she swallowed, causing her to cough.

Strawberry, a petite, extremely cute blonde haired, white girl, also swallowed her two packets. She gagged and brought one of the packets back up. She quickly caught her breath and swallowed the packet again.

A glass straight shooter slipped from Sheka's slim fingers and fell to the ground. She crushed it under the head of her powder blue Timberlands.

A voice shouted out, "Freeze, police! Put your hands on top of your heads and interlock your fingers."

Two uniformed police officers approached the ladies, one from each direction.

The girls froze. They placed their hands on top of their heads and the policemen roughly handcuffed them. The tall older balding white policeman pulled Sheka's cuffs up high, brushing her fingers against the front of his bulging trousers.

"Pervert!" she shouted. "What have we done?"

"We'll find out in a minute sweetie," said a short black cop with a thick mustache and a crooked smile.

Strawberry's mind was racing. She didn't want to go to jail. You couldn't get high in jail, and getting high was the only thing on her mind.

"We've been watching you two girls all night," smirked the white cop.

"Well, we went to my house and my mother was gone so we were locked out and didn't have no place to go. So we decided to walk around for a while. And..." Strawberry rattled on and on. Her eyes watered, her voice quivered.

Actually, she was pretty convincing.

The black cop led both girls to the rear of the patrol car parked closest to them.

"Is this the two girls that you told us about?" he asked as he leaned down speaking to someone sitting in the back seat.

A thin well-dressed white man sat with his hands cuffed behind his back. He stuck his narrow head out the window. He eyed them up and down.

"Yep, that's them. I fucked both of them. Heh, heh, and I gotta admit, it was worth it! Yeah, both of them for a hundred dollars was a steal!" Dude turned toward the white cop and asked, "You gonna let me go now?"

The white cop slammed the car shut. "Book them bitches, Phil. I'll take care of this weasel."

The thin man banged on the patrol car's window with his elbow. He started screaming inside the cruiser, "Hey! You promised. You fucking promised."

Phil started reading the girls their rights as he lead them back to his patrol car. Sheka mocked him by reciting the Miranda with him. She'd been arrested so many times that, *"the right to remain this and that,"* stuck with her.

Within minutes they were in the city jail. The Niagara Falls City Jail was really no more than a huge holding center. A wooden bench, a stainless steel toilet and a black plastic telephone receiver with a silver-grey panel with silver buttons hanging on the wall was what made up the 6x9 foot cell.

Strawberry picked up the black receiver and dialed her mother's number. *"This call is from Niagara Falls City Jail. This is an I.T.S. collect call. You may be billed as much as fifty cents for the first minute and twenty-five cents for each additional minute."* Strawberry hated how the jail phones told the world where you were, before you even had a chance to speak to anybody.

There was a long pause but no answer. She slammed the receiver back on its hook and lay down on the hard wooden bench. A chill swept over her. She rubbed her arms up and down trying to warm them. A tear fell from her eyes. She felt so lonely. She closed her eyes and slowly drifted off to sleep. Strawberry was awakened at 3:30PM, sharp. There was a lot of commotion going on in the cell block.

The officers were loading people into the transport van, getting them ready to take them to the county jail. Anybody that wasn't bailed out by 3:00PM went to county.

The ladies were tucked into the front of the van. A cage separated the area that the girls were seated from the rest of the van. There were a total of six girls.

A huge black girl with a buck-toothed smile sat next to Strawberry. An Indian girl with long jet black hair sat next to a fat older light-skinned black lady. Sheka sat next to an attractive slim white girl.

Once the ladies were loaded, the cage was locked. The rear door opened again and a dozen handcuffed men of all colors, shapes and sizes were ushered in. Whistles and catcalls filled the air. Most of the noise seemed to come from the caged women.

Sam, a tall black prisoner stopped and pulled a fresh pack of Newport 100's out of his pocket. He turned facing the white cop that was loading them, and asked, "Hey Joe, let me get a light man?"

Officer Joe pulled out a Marlboro and lit it, then lit the cigarette that was hanging from Sam's lips. Sam passed the pack round. Everyone took one. Even the women and guys that didn't smoke. This was their last act of freedom before they entered County. Almost everyone lit up and smoked. The ride was short and bumpy. Forty minutes later they pulled up in the city of Lockport. The Niagara County Jail.

The prisoners were herded in, stripped, bathed and searched. The matron that conducted the cavity searches had a permanent smile carved into her otherwise expressionless face. By the way that she went about her business, one could tell that she truly enjoyed her work.

She was a huge woman, weighing over three hundred and fifty pounds. Her hands were thick and her fingers were short and knobby, and she loved to probe.

The females were dressed and designated to pod B. Sheka was bunked with a skinny white girl with thick red hair and a face full of freckles. Strawberry was bunked with a two hundred and fifty pound black girl named Ollie.

The next morning at least a dozen of the girls in the pod were in front of Ollie's cell, welcoming her back. It appeared that Ollie had been in and out of jail often.

At breakfast, Sheka came over and sat with Strawberry. Strawberry was holding her stomach, and she looked extremely pale.

"Strawberry, I have to go. Do you have to go yet?" Sheka asked.

Strawberry laid her head on the table and closed her eyes. Sheka got up and went to the shower. She stripped quickly and turned the water on full blast. She pulled out her soap and began to lather up her body, paying extra attention to her round bottom. She stepped over to the doorway and peeked out. She was making sure that the C.O.'s and matron were still busy with the food trays.

Sheka eased a soaped up finger into her tight ass hole and began to pull down on it. She removed her finger but continued to push down hard. She repeated this action until she emptied her bowels on to the shower floor.

She stepped into the pile of shit and angled the shower spray on to her shit covered feet searching, feeling around with her toes.

"Aha!" she said as her toes ran across one of the plastic pockets, then the other. She continued to spray them with the shower head. She sprayed until her feet were clean and all of the feces was washed away. By the time she'd finished dressing, breakfast was over. Strawberry was lying on her bed moaning and holding her stomach.

"Strawberry, Strawberry!! Get up!! You've gotta get up and go to the bathroom. You've gotta *make* yourself go." Sheka grabbed her ailing friend and lifted her half way off the bed. Strawberry tried to stand on her own but fell to the hard tiled floor. Her body started to shake as convulsions over took her.

Tears started to pour down Sheka's face

"C.O.! C.O.!! Help us, please!" she cried. Other inmates began to gather around the cell, trying to see what was going on.

The unit C.O., a tall gangly man, ran over pushing his way through the crowd. He started as soon as he saw the convulsing girl twitching about on the floor.

"Shit! They said that this might happen!" He turned and ran back to his desk. He opened the bottom drawer and pulled out a quart sized plastic bag and about three feet of tubing. He applied a lubricant to one end of the tubing and barked, "Get her on her stomach and take those pants and panties off. This is going to get messy!"

Nobody moved.

"Damn it! Do what I say, and do it now. If you don't, she might die." The C.O. stood there holding the tube in one latex gloved hand and the plastic bag containing the liquid in the other.

Sheka and the petite white girl dropped to their knees, flipped the still shaking Strawberry over on to her stomach, and pulled off her orange pants and white panties.

"Hold her 'til I'm done!" he shouted. The officer bent down and slowly fed most of the tubing up Strawberry's vulnerable tight ass. She began to stir, trying to move away from the invading tube. The C.O. began to squeeze the liquid into her reddened butt, deep into her bowels. The door to the pad opened wide, and two huge black matrons came running in. The C.O. had just finished introducing the last of the liquid when one of the matrons knelt down beside him.

"Thanks Rick. We've got her now," the female officer said as Rick handed the empty bag to her and stepped back out of the way.

The matron looked down at the struggling petite girl and said, "OK sweetie, now comes the fun part."

They picked Strawberry up and sat her on the toilet. Then they removed the tubing and the fecal dam broke, filling the white commode. Two clear plastic bags could be seen floating in the water. Sheka grabbed a blanket to wrap around her shivering friend. One matron was holding Strawberry while another was wiping her behind. Sheka swung the blanket around Strawberry's shoulder and quickly flushed the toilet. Both matrons watched as the packets went down and out of the toilet.

Several more matrons came in and the C.O. left. The biggest, blackest of all the matrons stepped to the center of the pod. She pulled out a pair of latex medical gloves and a surgical mask. "OK ladies, line up and strip. This is gonna hurt me more than it hurts you!" She pulled the elastic on her wrist and snapped it. Big mama stared at her short fat fingers and smiled. "It's Showtime!" she exclaimed as she eagerly went about her work.

Chapter Two

Sheka was taken to special housing while Strawberry was taken to Medical.

Three days later, they were both returned to the pod without any evidence. The judge decided to let them go, and charges of introducing contraband were dropped. But both girls were sentenced to ninety days for loitering for the purpose of prostitution.

The first month went by quickly and without incident. Then sometime during the second month, Sheka and her bunky Amber were caught having sex. Both were given thirty days in the hole.

The first night that Sheka was gone, Strawberry was awakened from her sleep. Big Ollie pulled her down from her top bunk and stood before her, butt naked. She smiled at the sleepy white girl and said, "OK bitch, from now on your pretty little white ass belongs to me."

Ollie reached out and pulled Strawberry close, right up to her naked fat body. She forced their bodies to touch. She grabbed Strawberry's firm buttocks and almost lifted her from the ground. As Ollie pulled her closer Strawberry tried to get away, but she couldn't break the vice grip that Ollie had on her. Ollie tried to kiss Strawberry, but Strawberry turned her head away. Ollie grabbed the loose skin around Strawberry's side and twisted.

"Ow," Strawberry screamed out loud.

"Bitch, scream again and I will fuck you up!" Ollie growled. "Now strip!"

Strawberry resisted and slapped Ollie across the face.

"OK whitey, we'll do it your way."

The next morning Strawberry lay in bed crying. She wished that Sheka was there to help her the rest of the thirty days. The nights were too long and the days too short. She'd begun to obey Ollie's lust-filled requests, but Ollie would punish her anyway. Bruises and scratches marked her body. No matter what she did, Ollie found fault with it. Sometimes she'd fight, but she always lost. Every day Strawberry would make a little scratch on the wall. Last night made number 30. Finally Sheka and Amber were returned to the pod at breakfast on the thirty-first day. They were given separate rooms. Sheka walked around looking for Strawberry. She didn't see her. She walked over to her cell and saw Strawberry sound asleep in Ollie's bed. She walked in and shook her. "Strawberry, Strawberry! I'm back. Wake up and give your homegirl a hug."

Strawberry jumped up. "OK, OK, I'll do it! I'll do it!"

As Strawberry sat up, the blanket that covered her slid down to her waist. Black and blue marks covered her back. Both of her pert nipples were blue.

Tears welled up in Sheka's eyes. She touched her battered friend's face softly. A fire ignited inside of Sheka. The tears were now falling from Sheka's face onto the cold tiled floor. Sheka turned and ran out of the cell. She headed toward the dining area.

Strawberry covered herself with her blanket as best she could while screaming, "Sheka! Sheka, no! Don't Sheka! I'm OK. Really! I'm OK!"

But Sheka didn't stop. She ran over to the table where Big Ollie was busy stuffing her face from her third tray. Using both hands, Sheka picked up one of the empty trays and slammed it upside Ollie's fat face. Blood shot out of Ollie's flat broken nose. Again and again Sheka smashed the tray into Ollie's blood splattered face.

All of the girls at the surrounding tables stood up to block what was happening from the view of the C.O.

Sheka slipped around behind the much larger girl, grabbed a handful of greasy, nappy hair and pulled Ollie's massive, bleeding head back. She raised her fist high over her head and brought it down as hard as she could, slamming it into the fat girl's throat.

The huge girl fought to a standing position clutching her thick neck, gasping for air.

Sheka stepped to the side like she was performing a well rehearsed dance step and stomped hard into the back of one of Ollie's knees. Ollie toppled like a fallen Samoa tree. She hit the floor hard. Everyone began to scatter. The C.O. saw Ollie lying on the floor, but he didn't know why. He picked up his radio and called for backup.

Sheka began to kick and stomp the beached whale that was flopping around on the bloodstained floor. Suddenly, the door to the pod flew open. The goon squad ran in. A dozen women in full riot gear stood ready for war.

Someone blew a whistle. All of the female inmates scattered, running for the safety of their cells. Amber tugged at Sheka to get away. Strawberry was standing in the middle of the pod naked except for the blanket that she'd thrown around her.

A short freckle-faced red haired white girl named Jill, spit in Ollie's face as she pushed Strawberry, Amber and Sheka toward their cells.

The head matron who was the biggest and blackest of them walked over to where Ollie lay. She peered down at the badly beaten bully. "Well, well, well, it looks like the great big, bad Ollie finally got what she'd been asking for."

Ollie couldn't answer. She was still coughing and fighting to catch her breath.

The matron looked around. All of the girls were in their cells. She put her hands on her wide hips and asked, "I guess nobody saw what happened, huh?"

No one answered. The matron turned and waved to the waiting goon squad. "Come on, this one's over. Let's get superbitch here, over to medical."

Four of the largest goonies approached Ollie. Two grabbed her arms while two grabbed her legs. They half carried, half dragged Ollie's fat ass over to medical.

Soon the ninety days were up.

Tara and Teri, two of Sheka's Canadian friends, came to pick them up. Tara had borrowed a Nissan Pathfinder from one of her clients. Client was another name for her tricks.

Strawberry and Sheka squealed, hugged, kissed and cried. Everybody cried, then they went outside and hopped into the truck.

"I need to get high like right now," cried Sheka.

Tara froze. "Are you guys nuts. I mean like we are still sitting in the parking lot of Niagara County Jail. Am I the only sane person in here?" She started the truck.

Sheka opened the rear door. "Fuck that! I need to smoke." With that said, she hopped out of the truck and walked around the parking lot.

Tara closed her eyes as Sheka snapped the telescopic antenna off of a small black Ford. She ran back and climbed back into the truck.

"Find a store, I need some choi," Sheka demanded.

"Ugh!" screamed Tara. She beat her head on the steering wheel, then peeled off. Two blocks later, Tara whipped into the crowded parking lot of a Red Eagle Store.

Sheka snapped the antenna into two four-inch sections. The thinner section made a perfect push. She leaned up facing Tara and Teri. "OK, somebody go buy me some choi. And a Pepsi."

Nobody moved.

"Alright, I'll go in and steal it then."

Tara threw the car in Park and went inside of the store. Minutes later she came out carrying a small brown paper bag. She handed the bag to Sheka and climbed back into the truck.

Tara and Teri lit up a blunt that Teri had rolled while Sheka and Strawberry smoked some of the two grams of crack that Sheka had miraculously managed to hold on to.

Strawberry asked, "Sheka, where did you hide that shit? They shook us down and gave us cavity searches and shit. How did you manage to hide it?"

"I hid it up big Ollie's black ass!" answered Sheka. "I knew that matron's short fingers could never find it up all that ass!"

All four girls burst out laughing. To Tara and Teri, it sounded funny even though they didn't know Ollie. Strawberry sat there picturing what Sheka had just said. She imagined the fat black girl lying on her stomach as the portly matron probed around up into her wide ass, fingers just missing the packets.

Her mind quickly changed to the moment when Sheka beat the huge girl down. She sat back in the seat of the comfortable SUV, laid her head back and closed her eyes.

Where was her mother? Why hadn't she accepted her calls? Did her mother know it was her? Naw, she'd have accepted her call if she'd known it was her. Wouldn't she?

Chapter Three

Dancing Dave and his girlfriend Nina were moving fast. She was trying her best to keep up with him. Dave had just been served at a crack house on Cudabeck Street and was hurrying home to smoke.

Nina wore a long blue wool coat. Her collar was pulled up tight around her neck and her unkempt short hair was stuffed up under a red Yankee's baseball cap. Her dirty gray sneakers used to be white and were two sizes too large.

Nina's size nine jeans used to fit her tight. Her once bangin' ass was now flat and sagging. Her pancake breasts were once full, the size of grapefruit. Her face had become narrow, yet she was still cute.

Dave was tall, at least 6'2". He was once a star point guard on the old Trott Vocational High School basketball team. They were ranked third in the country and he'd been drafted by Georgetown University. John Thompson himself came to recruit Dave.

Success was too much for Dave. He couldn't handle all of the attention. He sought an escape. A friend had offered him some crack and he'd been smoking it ever since. Dave's boyish good looks had long ago grown into comic proportions. His nose had become more keen. His ears seemed larger than they used to be and protruded far from his neatly braided head. He also suffered from frequents bouts of paranoia.

Some of his old friends and others that remembered his past achievements would often pay him a few dollars to dance for them.

In his youth, Dave would dazzle everyone with his fancy footwork. But now, people would laugh and mock him as he jumped and twisted in the air, landing offbeat and often times off balance.

Today was a good day. He'd collected thirty bucks. He'd provide the high for that morning. Nina would go out on *'The patch'* later that evening, turn a couple of tricks and provide the high for them later on.

The couple hurried into the side door of an old red brick building. They stepped into a narrow hallway. A tall row of worn wooden stairs lay before them. A metal door stood beside them to their left. Dave bumped the door with his shoulder, opening it.

Inside was a sparsely furnished room. An old pink floral sofa sat on top of four evenly spaced cinder blocks. Mismatched coffee tables and end tables were placed neatly around the room. There was no television, no radio and no phone.

Nina reached under the sofa and pulled out her works. A five-inch glass straight shooter, choi, a push, one butane lighter, and some toilet tissue.

Good, she thought to herself. Everything was there. She packed the choi a little, using her push.

Dave pulled out a large piece of crack and broke off a piece which he gave to Nina. Her deft fingers fed the piece into the glass pipe. She picked up the altered butane lighter and flicked it. A bright yellow five-inch flame shot out and upward, lighting the pipe.

Nina inhaled deeply. She held the smoke as long as she could, then she shotgunned the smoke from her lungs into Dave's. Next it was Dave's turn. He duplicated the act. They continued until all of the crack was gone.

Dave got up and looked at the sun through the paper-covered front window. He guessed it to be about 4 pm. He leaned over and kissed Nina on the top of her head. It was more of a friendly kiss than one from a lover. "I'll be back soon, baby," he whispered into her ear.

Dave pulled the heavy metal door *hard* behind him as he left. He headed the fifteen blocks back up to the Elk's bar.

Nina sat on the sofa, scraping the side of her pipe for residue. Finally she gave up. There was nothing left to get. She put her works away and left, heading for the patch.

By seven o'clock Nina had turned four tricks. She smoked up half of the money, as was her custom. She kept a thirty-dollar piece to smoke with her man.

In minutes she was back at home. The apartment was dark. She felt around on the floor and found the end of an extension cord that ran from upstairs. She plugged a lamp into it. The darkness gave way to the dim light from the 40-watt bulb.

She called out. "Dave! Dave!"

There was no answer. Nina sat down and waited. Nine o'clock came and passed. Still, Dave hadn't come home. Nina pulled out her works and pinched off a tiny piece from her stash.

By ten o'clock the stash was gone, all smoked up. Dave still hadn't come home. Nina cut out the light and went back out to the Patch.

Dave was on his way up Highland Avenue. He'd just begun to cross over the Highland Street Bridge. The bar had been good to him. He held his forty dollars tight in his hand. The bills were folded as tight as he could make them.

Several young men in their late teens were walking toward him. Some were drinking forty ounces while others were smoking blunts.

Dave crossed to the other side of the street, trying to avoid a confrontation. Some of the young thugs crossed over to Dave's side of the road. One of the thugs called out to him.

"Hey, ain't you Dancin' Dave?"

"Yeah, that's him. I've seen him before. You guys should see him dance. It'll crack you up," shouted a short, muscular youth.

The thugs surrounded Dave. He stopped, debating whether he should run or not.

"Is that true Dave? Your name *is* Dave, right? Is it true Dave? Can you really dance like that?"

Dave didn't like the sound of their voices. Experience had taught him not to fuck with young guys, especially if they were high. He saw an opening and took off running back toward the safety of the bar.

The thugs took off after him. They chased him on both sides of the bridge.

Dave jumped over a guard rail and ran as fast as his forty year-old legs could carry him. But escape was impossible. The thugs had younger, stronger and faster legs. They easily caught up with the fiend and surrounded him.

A tall muscular youth wearing a dingy wife beater asked, "What the fuck you take off on us like that for, nigga?" The youth was bent over, resting his hands on his knees, breathing heavily.

Dave didn't answer. He knew that no matter what he said, it would be the wrong thing. So he stood there silently.

The rest of the youths caught up with them. A heavyset powerfully built youth with two gold teeth walked up to Dave. He took a long swig out of his forty ounce of Old English 800. His top lip curled. He looked awfully mean.

"Dance muthafucka! Dance! And you better be good 'cause if you ain't, I'm gon' fuck you up for making me and my boys run like that! Nigga!!"

He poked Dave hard in the chest. Dave knew that his only hope for survival was to entertain the young punks. He began to dance. He began to dance to a beat that only he could hear.

First he broke into the Robot, making jerky movements with his hands, legs and neck. The boys began to laugh. Dave dropped to the ground and began to kick his feet around, sometimes throwing them into the air, imitating a break dancer.

The boys began to boo.

The thug with the two gold teeth yelled out, "Is that all the fuck you got?"

Dave could tell that he was disappointing the youths. His eyes began to water.

One of the youths hauled off and hit Dave in the back of the head, knocking him to the ground. Several other thugs started kicking and stomping him. Dave tried to get to his feet, but every time he got up to his knees, somebody different would knock him back down.

All nine of the young men punched, kicked and stomped poor Dave. Dave took a powerful kick to the head. His body jerked as if he was trying to dance his way out of trouble. His bladder let loose, soaking his pants, then his body went limp. Still.

The men stopped their assault and turned, walking back down Highland. They left Dave as he lay. When the paramedics pulled up, Dave was already dead. He was still clutching the folded bills that he'd earned dancing at the Elks bar to buy crack for himself and his beloved Nina.

I was cruising through the patch looking for a quick blow job. Sometimes I could find one for as little as ten dollars. It was almost midnight.

A slim ho wearing a long blue wool coat and a red Yankees baseball cap scurried by. She was moving very fast.

I blinked the headlights on my car. She stopped. I pulled over and popped the locks. She hopped in. We dispensed with the formalities. We'd agreed on a ten dollar blow job.

Halfway through, she popped her head up and asked, "Look, can we fuck too? I need to make at least twenty-five dollars so that me and my man can smoke when I get home."

The head was bangin', but I obliged anyway.

Chapter Four

Friday, October 30th, 1998.

The wind and rain chased almost everyone off of the streets. I was cruising down 24th and Falls Street. It was 9:00pm, dark and dreary. The lights of my 1996 Lincoln were bouncing off of the telephone poles. A shadow moved. I slowed to a stop.

She stepped out in front of the limo. A tiny little thing. Her pale white complexion glowed. Her short pink skirt barely covered her buttocks. A black, short leather jacket was pulled tightly about her.

My dick began to rise. I hit the door locks, unlocking them. She opened the back door and jumped in. I could hear her feet sloshing in her soaking wet sneakers.

I pulled off and let down the dividers. The rearview mirror caught her trying her best to arrange her short skirt into a respectable position. She failed miserably.

"What's up?" I asked her as I gazed at the rearview mirror again. This time her white panties were visible. A white vee was clearly showing under her pink skirt.

She crossed her slim, shapely legs. Her small fingers were busy stroking her long blonde hair. She caught me staring at the mirror and slid up the J seat of the limo, stopping at the lowered divider. She leaned through the window, resting her chin on the damp leather sleeve of her coat.

"You're not a cop are you? 'Cause if you are, you can let me out right here. I'm on my way to my mother's house."

"Cut the crap, baby. No, I'm not a cop. Are you?" I had to ask. Sometimes nice looking cops pose as prostitutes to catch unsuspecting Johns.

She laughed and answered "No baby, I'm a lot of things, but a cop ain't one of them."

I turned down Buffalo Avenue to Tenth Street, turning again on Tenth. I pulled under an underpass and stopped. We were in a very secluded section of the road. I got out of the car, opened the back door and slid in next to her.

"What's your name, sweetie?" I asked

"They call me Strawberry. What's yours?"

"They call me Niggah. But not to my face. What's your real name?"

"My real name is for friends and family only, and I would never call you the "N" word. So, what do the other girls call you?"

"Other girls?"

"Sure, *other* girls! You're sort of cute. I know that there are plenty of other girls. What do they call you?"

I sat up closer to her smiling. "They call me Chris. My name is Christopher."

Strawberry extended her hand. "Glad to meet you, Chris."

We shook hands. "Glad to meet you too, Strawberry," I said.

Strawberry's hand was so tiny, so soft and so white. Our hands lingered like that for a second.

"Nice ring, Chris."

Damnit! I had meant to take my 1.5 carat pinky ring off my finger and put it in my pocket. You should never let a ho know you have money. I eased my Rolex up under the sleeve of my tuxedo jacket. "Thank you," I answered. "Now, let's get down to business. How much?"

"Twenty for head. No cumming in my mouth. For fifty, we can fuck too. Do you have any condoms?"

She rattled the words off as if she'd said them over a thousand times. She opened up her leather jacket so that I could get a better look at the goods.

Nice tits, a small waist, real shapely slim legs. I wanted to fuck. To fuck her petite brains out. "OK, fifty, but not here."

I got out of the car. A brown Dodge Caravan was creeping down the street, obviously looking for a ho.

I nodded as they passed. *Too late,* I laughed, *I got mine.* I jumped behind the wheel, started the car, eased the long limo back into the street and headed home.

I lived in a lime green vinyl sided bungalow at 221 59th Street. I parked in front of the house. I got out and opened the door for Strawberry. The street was so quiet that I could hear my dog rustling around, sniffing the air as I walked my little Strawberry into my house. She stood in the doorway while I cut on the lights.

"Take those wet shoes off. I don't want to soak the carpet," I commanded. I helped her out of her coat and she stepped out of her soggy sneakers.

"Chris, are you gonna take me back when we're done. I don't usually come this far out, you know what I mean?"

I laughed out loud. "Yeah! I know what you mean. I'll get you back, don't worry."

She stood at the entrance to the living room staring at the white embroidered French provincial furniture. The dark oak trimming had just been polished and was glistening under the lights. I went upstairs and took off my tuxedo. I grabbed my blue robe, threw it on, and grabbed a pink one that I'd kept for female guests.

When I got downstairs Strawberry was still standing in the entrance to the living room. I handed her the pink robe.

"Here, take those wet clothes off. I'll wash and dry them for you."

She shivered as she began to disrobe.

It was sort of cool, so I started a fire in the fireplace. Strawberry undressed quickly and joined me on the faux tiger skin rug that was spread in front of the fireplace. We both sat there watching the flames dance and leap across the fireplace,

"Chris, would you mind if I showered first?"

"No baby, you go right ahead. The bathroom is at the top of the stairs. I'll throw your clothes in the wash while you shower."

She got up and went upstairs. Her right hand was shoved deep into the pocket of her robe. Then it hit me. *She had needed to smoke*. Why else would a pretty little white girl like her be out turning tricks in the hood. *Crack!* I gathered up her clothes - a short pink skirt, a thin white blouse, white bikini panties, no bra, no socks and the dripping sneakers.

The sound of water shooting from the shower started. I took the clothes down to the basement and started the washer. I threw everything in at once and went back and sat in front of the fire.

When Strawberry came downstairs, she looked different-fresh, clean, almost innocent. She even looked younger. She walked over, stood behind me and put her arms around my neck.

I reached behind me. My fingers climbed up under her robe and on to her firm thigh. She didn't flinch a muscle. Instead, she began to conversate.

"Do you live here alone, Chris?"

"Not really, I live here with my two watch dogs. I only let them meet special people. You understand, don't you?"

"This is a real nice house. A girl could grow to like living in a house like this." The comment was meant to be nonchalant, but her eyes deceived her as they continued to circle the room. They came to rest on a huge 24-inch picture of several children and two very large dogs.

"Who are the kids, Chris?"

"They're mine."

"All of them?"

"You ask too many questions!" I blurted. I reached into my robe pocket and pulled out a crisp new fifty-dollar bill, which I handed to her.

She took the hint and shut up. She untied the robe and let it slide down her narrow shoulders. I pulled her around in front of me. *Damn! This bitch was fine!* Her pert ripe breasts set out in front of her like fog lights on a Chevy Blazer.

I pulled a condom out of my other pocket and handed it to her. She politely took it and opened it. She pushed it into her mouth and pushed me back on to the floor. Her slender, experienced fingers untied and removed my robe. My rock hard dick stood straight up like a soldier standing at attention. She lowered her head; blond tresses teased my groin as she completely engulfed my dick.

Fuck! Her warm mouth felt too damn good! Even with the condom on, she had an excellent head game. I lay there enjoying her work. Then without warning, she straddled me. Reverse cowgirl. She rode and rode and rode. Grabbing the cheek of her firm round behind, I slammed her down hard on my hard dick.

She yelped like a hurt puppy. Her sounds only made me fuck into her harder. I tried to ram my dick up through her body, but she took it all. She turned and faced me as she rode. I could feel my balls starting to swell. Preparing to explode inside her, I pushed her off and turned her around on her hands and knees. Doggy style. I entered her from behind. I pounded her tight pussy as hard and as fast as I could. I wanted to punish her pussy.

She screamed out loud. "Oh my God! Oh My God! Why are you fucking me like this? Why?"

I was too engrossed to talk. I actually tried to eviscerate her, using my dick as the tool.

And then I came. I came with the force of an erupting Mt. St. Helens. She began to tremble and shake all over. She closed her eyes. A redness appeared across the top of her chest. Her nipples were erect. Her breathing became erratic. The spurts from my dick had ceased. Contractions like tiny fingers continued to milk my softening penis.

I fell over onto my side, exhausted totally.

She curled up next to me, resting her head on my chest.

The fire crackled and popped. Shadows danced across the wall. We lay like that for a good while. The scent of sex still stirred my nose.

"Chris?"

"Yeah!"

"Are you sleeping?"

"No, I was just catching my breath. I'm not as young as I used to be."

"Chris, you're different."

"Hmm? Different. Different how?"

She turned and rested her pretty little head between her hands, while resting her elbows on the tiger skin rug. "You're different from anyone else that I've ever been with. You're nice...real nice."

There was a moment of silence. She drew circles on my chest with her fingers.

"Chris, why are you so nice to me? Huh?"

"Why shouldn't I be nice? That was a hell-of-a work out you gave me."

We both laughed. I could have sworn that she blushed. I sat up, wrapped my robe around me and went downstairs to put her clothes in the dryer.

When I came back in the living room, she had put the pink robe back on her, and her hand was stuffed deep down in one of the pockets.

"Are you hungry?" I asked.

"Um, no thank you. Do you have something to drink?" she asked.

"Sure, what will you have? Cognac, Gin, Whiskey, Vodka, Wine?"

"Uh! I meant a soda. Do you have a Pepsi?"

"My bad. I'll get you a Pepsi."

I got up and got two Pepsi's from the fridge. She got up and followed me. I twisted off the cap and handed a cold one to her.

She turned the bottle up and guzzled half of the cold soda down. "Ahh!" She burped out loud and laughed.

I liked the sound of her laughter. There hadn't been any laughter in my house in quite some time.

"Strawberry? Why is someone as young, fine and fun as you are, out there selling your ass for a few pennies?"

She turned her head away. Then stared at the floor.

"I'm a strawberry Chris. Do you know what a strawberry is?"

I shook my head no. I was up on most street jargon, but I hadn't heard this term. I for one knew that I was what one called a *Window Shopper*. And although a Window Shopper could be anything by individual perception and understanding, I was one because of my hustle for tricks. I'd fly around in one of my vehicles, tucked most of the time behind some dark tint and *shop*, through my window.

She continued, "A strawberry is a female crackhead. I turn tricks to get high. I'll take the dope *or* the money. It doesn't matter. They call us strawberries because we parade around, up and down the street. Easy pickings for anybody willing to pay us. Anybody's bitch for the moment.'

I didn't know what to say. She was so blunt. I went back into the living room and put another quick light log in the fire. We both sat down in front of it saying nothing.

My cell phone rang. I answered, "Nubian Chariot Limousine Service. How may I help you?"

"Yo, Yeah, dig. I need a car for tonight. You copy?" came a smooth male voice.

"Uh, why yes, I copy. How long will you need it and for how many people?"

"Well, let me see...Solo, Sears, Boo, Moe and me. It'll be five or six of us. We want to hit the Casino Niagara and a couple of strip clubs so we can fuck with some snow bunnies. Probably six hours."

"That'll be three hundred dollars for my special late night rate. What time would you like the car to arrive?"

"Is an hour from now cool?"

"I'll be there in an hour. Who shall I ask for?"

"Ask for Geno. That's me."

"See you in an hour, Geno."

I hung up the phone and looked at my watch. It was eleven o'clock sharp. When I looked up Strawberry was standing in front of me.

"I know Chris. It's time for me to go. I understand. It's business."

I went and got her clothes. The sneakers were still damp. I went upstairs, showered and dressed. We didn't talk much as I drove her back to 24th Street. I didn't quite know what to say. I dropped Strawberry off on the corner of 24th and Cudabeck. There was a popular crack house down the street.

I quickly cleaned the inside of the limo, put ice in the cooler, chilled a bottle of Andre's Champagne and lit a black cherry incense. By the time I was done it was time to pick up my fare.

The address was 707 Elmwood Avenue. I pulled up and blew the horn once. A bald light-skinned pretty nigga came out of the house followed by four other young fellows. I jumped out and opened the door for them. Geno turned the stereo on to WBLK, the area's black radio station.

I took them to the Casino Niagara, then to Mints, The Sundowner and finally Seductions Strip Clubs. By six o'clock I was beat. I pulled in front of their house and was barely able to get out and open the door for them. Geno handed me four one hundred dollar bills. I thanked him and headed home.

I pulled up in front of my house and parked. Sitting on the stairs, all balled up, still wearing the short pink skirt, was Strawberry. I walked over to her. I was furious. I started yelling at her before I was within ten feet of her. "Look bitch, I don't want you coming around my house whenever you need a hit."

Strawberry stood to walk away. She kept her face tucked down as if to hide it. She bumped into me as she passed. A huge bruise covered the entire left side of her face. I reached out and grabbed her by the arm. She winced in pain. I quickly let her go. Her blouse hung open. The buttons were gone. I put a finger under her chin and raised her face. Her left eye was closed. The right one wasn't much better. Tears flowed from both. She pulled away and started to walk down the remainder of the walkway.

I called out to her "Strawberry! Wait!" I didn't know what else to call her.

She stopped but continued facing the street.

"Let me take you to the hospital? That eye looks real bad." I asked

"I can't go to the hospital... police... questions...I can't."

I walked up and opened the front door. "Strawberry, are you coming? Or do I have to carry you in?" I stood there holding the door open.

She slowly turned and walked inside the house.

Chapter Five

Two weeks had passed since the memorable night that I came home and found my little Strawberry all curled up on my doorstep. I bathed her and applied cold compresses to her eye.

She was pretty beat up. She pretty much slept the first three days away. Waking only to eat and use the bathroom. The fourth day I found her sitting up in bed watching television.

"Hey! It's good to see you up. Feeling better?"

She shrugged her shoulders and kept watching the television. I walked over and sat on the edge of the bed. I stroked her hair. It flowed through my fingers. I'd brushed it every day while she slept.

"Do you want to talk about it?" I asked.

Tears welled up in her eyes. She remained silent. I picked up the remote control and turned the TV off. The tears began to flow as she thought back to that night. The night we met.

"They didn't have to do me like that. They didn't have to." She wiped the tears from her eyes and sniffed up real hard as she began to tell me her story. This is what she said:

She went to a crack house to spend the fifty dollars that I'd just given her. It was her regular dope guy. A dude that usually served her swell. Well, he gave her a thirty-five for the fifty. She knew that he was playing her, but she didn't care because homeboy's shit was usually Flav.

Dude allowed her to go into one of his back rooms to smoke like she always did. Twenty minutes later ol' boy burst into the room and screamed on her, "Bitch, who the fuck you think you playin'? This bill is counterfeit. I want some real money, now! Or I want my shit back."

Strawberry was startled. She'd smoked up half of the maniac's shit and didn't have any more money. "I don't have any more money. That fifty was all I had. There's got to be some kinda mistake. That money's good. I checked it myself," she pleaded.

Dude tossed a phony fifty-dollar bill on the floor. Strawberry picked it up and examined it.

"This ain't the fifty that I gave you. The one I gave you was new."

"Bitch, you callin' me a lie! In my own house!" Homie stepped up. He was well over six feet tall. He reached out and grabbed Strawberry around her neck. "You fuckin' white assed ho! You owe me fifty dollars worth of shit. I want some money or I want some ass!" He threatened.

"Me too, I want some of the snow bunnie's ass too," shouted one of the friends that was sitting on homeboy's sofa. Both men jumped up. One of them checked the blankets that covered the window. The other locked the door.

Dude unzipped his pants and pulled out his semi-hard dick. He forced Strawberry's head down to it. His dick pounced off of her closed mouth.

Dude pulled her upright. "So you don't want to play, huh?" he asked before lifting his knee fast and hard. It caught her in the stomach, causing her to double over in pain. She screamed. Dude started punching her in the face, trying to shut her up. One punch caught the left side of her face knocking her to the floor. Her screaming ceased.

Strawberry rose to her knees, still holding on to what was left of her dope. She opened her mouth and Dude rammed his dick down her throat causing her to choke. Her mouth hurt, but she started sucking his long hard dick, hoping that he'd come real soon.

His friends were goading him on. He came quick, pulling out of her mouth and shooting all over her face and hair. All three men were laughing. Strawberry attempted to get up off of her sore knees.

"Where do you think you're going, *snow bunny*? I ain't had mines yet." This was the tallest of the three. He smiled showing off a complete set of gold teeth. His incisors were extended like Dracula's.

The three men grabbed Strawberry and lifted her up off the floor. They draped her over an ottoman that sat in the middle of the floor; her pink skirt was riding around her waist. She kicked and struggled as hard as she could, but it was fruitless. Someone ripped her white bikini panties off of her tanned body.

The tall man with the gold mouth unzipped his pants and plunged into her tight pussy from behind. He fucked and fucked her unwilling cunt. It seemed to last forever. Finally he came. His hot seminal fluid seemed to sear her insides. He pulled out and wiped himself clean on her bunched up skirt.

The third man walked up behind her. She could feel him standing over her. He, too, was tall, but he had perfect white teeth and his hair was braided into two shoulder length braids.

"I ain't never had no white meat before. Maybe I need to tenderize it first," he stated as he pulled his long, wide belt from his pants. He doubled it and started beating her lily white ass.

The more he hit her, the more he craved to beat her. Sweat covered his brow, dripping all over her. Harder and harder he swung. He started talking to her, explaining why as he continued to swing.

"And this is for all the black men that your father's beat. And this is for all the beautiful black women that your fathers raped. And this is for…" he went on and on and on.

Dude finally stopped him. "Come on man, do what you gotta do so we can dump this tramp."

The tall man dropped his belt. Sweat poured from his body. He unzipped his pants and stood there behind her badly welted body, catching his breath. Then he uttered between deep breaths, "Hey man, do you have any grease?"

Dude laughed and said. "Naw man, I ain't got no… wait a minute…yeah, I do. Hold up."

Dude went into the kitchen and returned with a can of butter flavored Crisco in his hand.

The man with the braids said, "You gotta be kidding?"

"Naw man, that's all I have. Now do what you gotta do."

The braid-wearing cat shook his head and stuck his hand deep into the golden yellow Crisco. He applied an ample amount to his dick and to Strawberry's ass.

She pressed her face into the ottoman, knowing that she couldn't prevent what was about to happen.

He fucked her ass long and hard. He fucked with reckless abandon. Four hundred years of racial hatred poured through his dick.

And when he erupted he screamed, finally gaining some of the vengeance he'd sought all his life. He stepped in front of her and grabbed her by her hair, forcing his shit stained dick into her still bleeding mouth.

She gagged on his shit tasting dick.

Dude snatched her up off the floor like a child might lift a doll. He carried her out on the front porch and tossed her out on the lawn.

It was pouring raining. She lay there, enjoying the rain's coolness.

Someone tossed her her coat and ripped up white panties. Somebody began to urinate on her. She was too beat to look up. Someone hocked up a mouthful of spit and heaved it in the back of her head.

"Damn man, I need a blunt," said Dude as he wiped his mouth with the back of his hand. They all went back into the house, patting each other on the backs and dropping dap.

A half an hour went by before Strawberry could force herself to her feet and start walking. She walked blindly around the city, ignoring the rain, the wind and the cold, up and down the winding streets.

She didn't want to go back to the apartment that she sometimes slept at. There were four other crackhead girls there, and she couldn't deal with them at the moment.

She started walking towards 59th Street, my house. It was only an hour away. She sat on my step for over three hours.

After she told me her story, I became angry. I wanted to hurt those men for hurting her. But then I remembered the code of the street. One Black man never raises his hand to another Black man over a white girl. Never!

Chapter Six

I learned that Brigette Duquense was from Montreal, Quebec, way up in Canada. She came down to the States two years ago. Her mother had met a man that lived in the states. She'd fallen in love with him and wanted to be closer to him.

Sometimes her mother would be gone for weeks at a time. The food in the house would run out. The telephone and lights would be turned off. And the lecherous landlord would threaten to throw Strawberry out into the streets if she didn't perform certain sex acts with him.

She would always refuse him. Then one night, he threw her out. She didn't know where to go. She walked the street for two nights. On the third night she met an older streetwise girl named Tiffany.

Tiffany fed her and let her crash at her place. They would drink and smoke weed together. Then one day Strawberry asked Tiffany how show got her money. It was obvious that she didn't have a job.

Tiffany took her out to the patch. Strawberry turned her first trick and eventually hit the pipe for the first time as well. She'd been smoking and tricking ever since.

Then Tiffany got busted and went to jail for six months. Strawberry picked up the slack. Now she had to trick to pay bills as well as to provide for her high.

But it got to be more than she cared to bear. She met Tara, a beautiful mulatto from St. Catherine's, Ontario. Tara danced at the Canadian Strip clubs. Tara shared an apartment with two other girls. Jennifer, a short beautiful mixture of Italian and Puerto Rican, and Tynesha, a mixture of black, white and Indian. They allowed Strawberry to stay with them. The apartment next door to them was occupied by several white girls from Canada.

I took Strawberry home one day to get some clothes. All three of her roommates were there. They were wearing panties and bras or sheer housecoats that they refused to button.

They were all so fuckin' beautiful! I had to sit down and cross a leg to hide my erection. I was extremely uncomfortable and the girls seemed to sense it and play up on it.

I was glad when we left. I took Strawberry back to the house. I introduced her to General, a shepherd-alaskan malamute mix and Sarge, a purebred shepherd. She had a knack with dogs. They took to her immediately.

When she finally came into the house to shower, I joined her. We made love there and again in bed. In the morning we made love on the kitchen counter and again in the basement with her legs wrapped around my waist and her buttocks bouncing off of the running dryer.

For the next month, we would make love three to four times a day. I was whipped. Totally, beautifully whipped. All I thought about was her. I didn't want to leave her in the mornings, and I hurried home to her at night. Work was becoming a terrible inconvenience.

I left one morning to go to work. By noon I was missing my little Strawberry too much. I left and burned up the road heading home.

When I got there, the house was empty. The dogs were running around in the backyard, but she was gone. The backdoor was unlocked. She must have left it that way so she could get back in. I still hadn't given her a key to the house.

I went upstairs and showered and shaved. I searched the cabinets for my beard trimmers. They weren't there. I went into my bedroom looking for my trimmers. I noticed that the door to the guest room was open. I went over and pushed the door open. I looked around the room. Then it hit me. The 19-inch color television was gone.

I heard the sound of the backdoor opening and closing. Angrily, I ran down the stairs and into the kitchen. Strawberry was sitting in a chair. The 19-inch TV was on the table next to her.

Her head was down on the table. She was crying into her arms.

"Fuck those tears! How could you steal from me?" I screamed, "And where the fuck are my beard trimmers?"

She cried louder, letting me know that they were gone.

I grabbed the TV getting ready to take it back upstairs. I noticed that the toaster and crock pot were gone. I sat the TV down and grabbed her by her long blond hair. I half led, half dragged her to the front door.

She started screaming, "Chris! I couldn't sell it! I couldn't sell it! I brought it back. Wait Chris! Wait!"

I didn't know what the fuck I was thinking. Bringing a ho into my house like this? I started screaming at her as I tossed her ass out of the front door. "You can't change a fuckin' crackhead! You gotta let a ho be a ho."

I slammed the door and locked it. I ran and locked the back door too. I could hear her beating on the front door, pleading, begging for me to let her back in.

I went upstairs and went to sleep. When I woke up the next morning, Strawberry was gone. I went through the house from top to bottom. Seeing what else that bitch might have taken. Most of my power tools were gone, drills, saws, wrenches. Even my power mower. I got dressed for work. *How could I have been so fuckin' dumb?*

Chapter Seven

I tricked with just about every ho in the Falls. People kept trying to hook me up with different nice young ladies, but I wasn't interested. All I wanted was sex. I was trying my best to fuck Strawberry out of mind.

But nothing seemed to work. A friend told me about a beautiful young lady named Nae Nae. He bragged about her for so long that I felt compelled to call her.

Her voice was angelic and when I first laid my eyes on her, I had to pinch myself to make sure that I wasn't dreaming. We hit it off great, but then my drinking interfered with our relationship. She left me, or should I say, that I drove her away.

Strawberry came back around, and we both entered rehabs. She'd gotten pregnant and had our love child, Tatiana. Everything was perfect. And then one day my Strawberry was gone again.

It took awhile and a lot of ass kissing to get Nae Nae back, but she came back. Now we are married and have a child of our own, little Jessica.

Geno's crew got hit. Sears and Boo got killed. Solo and Moe got hit with ten years each and were sent to Federal prison. Eventually Geno quit dealing and bought into the limo business with me.

I am still baffled by the hypnotic draw of young intelligent women into the Patch. Even Freddy, my manager, was sucking dicks to pay for his high. He too is now clean and sober.

For the most part, I'm happy. I've got a beautiful, intelligent wife, two adorable little girls, a booming business, and strong clean friends. I've got everything that a man can ask for and remain reasonably happy. I'm finally at the point where I only think about Strawberry every now and then. She no longer occupies my mind.

Nae Nae has stepped up and become a wonderful mother to Tatiana, and the perfect wife to me. I sometimes wonder, what did I do to deserve her?

We still have little problems like I guess all couples do. I didn't want her to work. That only lasted 'til Jessica was six months old. Nae Nae is too independent to sit at home.

I still drive every now and then. I like driving. I get to ride all over the city. I meet new people almost daily. And I make good money, *Window Shopping.*

It gives me a chance to clear my head. To get away from my own world and enter the world of hoes, dope dealers and hustlers of every kind. I'm on my way to a job tonight. I hadn't gone out on a job in a couple of weeks.

The parking lot of the Casino Seneca was filled. A new 16-story 4-star hotel had been built adjacent to it. Another hotel and a new convention center had also been added to the city. The last five years had hundreds of millions of dollars invested in a wide variety of businesses. Niagara Falls was a city on the move.

Money was everywhere. Everybody from the hotel investors to the street vendors were in on the money. The police force had been increased by twenty, their salaries paid out of the increase of tax revenue that was generated by the hotels, convention center and Casino.

A special task force was developed to rid the areas near the casino of prostitutes. An outbreak of Syphilis in 2004 prompted the formation of the task force. The entire area from 18th Street down to the Falls was cleaned up. All small time crack dealers and cheap hoes were gone. It was strange riding down the strawberry patch at midnight and finding it lit up with lights and void of people.

I turned my 22-passenger stretch Hummer left, heading down toward Highland Avenue. Highland was the all-Black part of the city. All of the hoes and most of the dope were transferred to the Black area. I pulled out the contract. *1069 Highland Avenue, 284-1864, Pervis.* I punched the number in on my cell phone and slowed the Hummer to a roll.

A tall, buxom, dark-skinned ho with legs up to her neck, stepped in front of the truck. The phone continued to ring. "You lonely boss?" asked the dark-skinned ho.

I looked up at her mesmerizing smile. "Not interested," I lied. I was *very* interested. But I had Nae Nae at home. Ever since Brigette left, I'd remained faithful to Nae Nae.

The ho turned and flicked up the bottom of her extremely short skirt at me. She wore nothing underneath.

"Damn," I said to myself. "Damn, that bitch is hot as fuck, and she knows it too!"

The phone stopped ringing, "Hello?"

"Hello, Perv speaking."

"This is the limousine service calling. I'm right outside of your house."

"Cool. We'll be right out." *Click.*

A door opened across the street. An entourage of people poured out and into the Hummer as I stood at its side, holding the door open. Six men and six women piled into the luxury vehicle.

"Yo, Driver, to the Addams Mark in Buffalo."

I assumed that the dark man with the Colgate smile, giving me directions was Pervis.

The sharp acrid aroma of freshly rolled blunts slowly filled the air. The sounds of *The Game* vibrated off the DVD system. Two loud *"pops"* from behind the closed divider told me that the bubbly was being passed.

I hit I-90 off of the boulevard and opened up heading south to Buffalo. It was a clear cool night. The road was almost bare. Twenty minutes flat and I rolled up in the circular drive at the mark. They were featuring an amateur comedy night. I opened the door and helped everyone exit. I pulled around the corner and found several other limousines parked there. I pulled up behind the last one, parked and joined the other drivers that were standing at a bus stop smoking.

I could smell the stench of commercial weed. Two young white girls walked past us. One wore a tiny pink skirt and a short black leather jacket.

Images of Brigette flashed through my mind. The other girl was tall, slim and blonde. Just like Brigette's friend Tiffany.

Some of the chauffers whistled and shouted obscenities at the pair as they passed.

I wondered how Brigette was doing. *Where was she? Did she ever think of me? Did she ever really care?* Foolish questions...

After the show ended I took the crowd to Three Brother's bar on Highland and College Avenues. Pervis said that they would be there for at least two hours.

I parked on the side of the building. It seemed that every person that passed stopped and stared at the huge Hummer, wondering what Celebrity might be inside.

I called home, Nae Nae answered. "Hello?"

"Hey baby it's me."

"Hey Chris, where are you?"

"I'm at the club on Highland. I'm still with the fare. How's the kids?"

"Tatiana is sleeping and Jessica is laying here next to me wide awake. I really believe that she feels that she has to wait on you to come home before she can sleep."

"That's my girl. Give her the phone for a moment."

Nae Nae handed Jessica the phone "Hi daddy!"

"Hey babygirl. Do you miss me?"

"Come home daddy. Come home right now!"

I burst out laughing. "Give the phone back to mommy, baby."

Jessica obediently handed the phone back to her mother.

"OK Chris, how much longer do you think you'll be?"

"At least another two hours baby. But I'll be there just as soon as they're done."

"OK, I love, you Chris."

"I love you too, baby. Bye."

Damn. Alone again. All these years clean and sober and I still hated being alone. I started up the big Hummer and pulled off down College Avenue.

I took College to Lewiston Avenue, which turned into Main Street. Cruising up Main Street, a woman ran up to the truck and started beating on the truck's hood.

"Help me! Please help me! They'll kill me if they catch me," she shouted, still holding onto the hood.

Two tall young black men came running out of the building on the corner. They looked in our direction and started walking toward us. They looked serious. I didn't want to get involved, but the woman wouldn't let go of the door.

I popped open the door locks and she jumped in. Smoke rose from the tires as I floored the accelerator. The light at South and Main changed red. I went through it as if it weren't even there.

We flew down Main to Pine. We turned left and slowed down as we went up Pine. I lowered the divider so I could interrogate my passenger.

"We're safe now. What's your name?"

She smiled as she answered, "Have I changed that much that you don't know who I am, Chris?"

I couldn't believe my ears. Naw, there had to be some kinda mistake. "Tiffany? Brigette's friend Tiffany?"

"Of course, Chris. It's me." She hopped from one seat to the closest one to the divider. She crawled through the divider headfirst. Her skimpy black skirt failed to hide her black thong and her still pleasing ass. She sat up next to me and straightened out her clothes. Definitely false modesty. The Tiffany that I knew was more comfortable naked than clothed. She pulled a Newport out of her pocket. No purse. No cigarette pack. Still buying loosies.

She pulled a lighter out of her pocket and lit the cigarette on the four-inch flame.

I didn't need to ask. She was still smoking crack. Now I was beginning to wish that I hadn't saved her sorry ass. I ain't no captain-save-a-ho. I pulled over and stopped.

"OK, you're safe. You can get out now."

"What's the matter Chris? Do I make you nervous? Come on admit it. Admit that you enjoyed fucking me in the ass. Do you want to hop in the back and fuck me up the ass right now, Chris? Come on. This one's on me."

She turned and tried to climb back through the divider. I reached out, grabbed her around her tiny waist and pulled. She landed in my lap. Her firm buttocks surrounded my growing penis. She could feel my dick growing under her. She ground down, hard against my groin. "Tiffany, stop!!" I shouted. "Please, leave my truck please?"

Tiffany got off of my lap and resumed her seat next to me. Staring at her feet, she asked, "Have you seen or heard from her?"

"No, No I haven't. Have you?"

"Would you like to hear from her?"

The question bounced all through my head. *Of course I wanted to see her, but how? And then what?*

Tiffany opened the door and stepped out. "Bye Chris," was all that she said before she closed the door and walked away. I wanted to call her back. But I didn't.

I drove back to the bar to wait on my fare. I closed my eyes, remembering the first time that I'd met her, the first time that I told her that I loved her, our first night, Tatiana's birth, her mother's death, her disappearance.

I wondered.

Chapter Eight

Tiffany walked down Tenth Street, looking back behind her every now and then. It was as if she knew that she was being followed. Yet, she saw no one.

Home at last. She turned and entered an area between two buildings. The side door was unlocked. She ran up to the third floor. Her deft fingers found her key and quickly opened the door.

Without turning on a light she pulled a cell phone out of a brown paper bag that lay in the kitchen trash can and punched in several digits.

"Hello."

"Hey, it's me."

"Tiffany? What up?"

"I just left him."

"Left who?"

"Left Chris, you dummy."

"Oh yeah. How is he? How'd he look? Where'd you see him?"

"He's fine and he looked cute as ever. He's doing real good for himself. He added a stretch Hummer to his fleet."

"God I wish I could see him."

"You can. All you have to do is come back. You can stay with me."

"You know that I can't stay there. I've been clean for eighteen months. I'd throw that all out the window if I came and stayed with you."

"Well suit yourself. I just wanted to let you know that I saw him."

There was silence on the other end. Then; "Tiffany. Did you? Did he?"

"Girl p-l-e-a-s-e. No he didn't touch me and believe me, I tried. And no, he didn't ask about you. I sorta brought your name up. But I can tell you this. His whole face lit up when I mentioned you."

"Really?"

"Really," answered Tiffany in a mocking fashion.

Suddenly the door burst open! Tiffany jumped up to run, but one of the men grabbed her around her waist, lifted her high into the air and slammed her to the floor. Tiffany bounced like a basketball. The cell phone fell from her hand.

"Thought you was slick, huh bitch. Where the fuck is my shit? I want every fuckin' rock!! And I want all of my shit right now!!!"

Tiffany tried to get up, but a kick to the side of her head knocked her back to the floor.

"Bitch, I said that I want my shit!"

Tiffany felt inside of her coat pocket. Empty!! She dug her hand deeper, but the pocket was empty. She panicked. It was only four buck packs that she'd stolen, but she had absolutely no means whatsoever to pay for it.

One of the three men, a brute of a beast, grabbed Tiffany by the neck. She wanted to scream. She needed to breathe. But she could do neither. She struggled for air. Her short skirt was wrapped around her waist. The sight of her thong covered ass gave Black an idea.

"T-Bone, Cleve, pick her bitch ass up and stick a sock in her mouth. I'm going to the car to get Bruno."

Black went downstairs and got Bruno out of the car. Bruno was a beautiful eighty-five pound red nosed tawny pit bull. Black opened the trunk and pulled an 8mm camcorder out of the trunk.

T-Bone turned one of the kitchen chairs over. It resembled a man on his knees. They secured Tiffany to the chair legs. Cleve pulled up her skirt and tore her panties off.

Pow! Cleve spanked her ass. "Yeah man, this shit is ripe." Cleve unzipped his pants and entered Tiffany's upturned ass. Cleve was fucking the shit out of her when Black and Bruno came in.

"Damn Cleve! You started without us."

Cleve continued his punishing dick attack.

"Here, start filming." Black tossed the camcorder to T-Bone who instantly started filming. Cleve played for the camera. He picked up his assault.

Brigette was still listening from the other end of the cell phone that still lay on the kitchen floor. *Is that a dog barking?* Her mind was trying to piece together what might be transpiring with Tiffany.

When Cleve was done, he shot cum all over her round sore ass.

Black led Bruno up to Tiffany's cum soaked ass. Bruno stuck his cold nose up Tiffany's ass. He hungrily lapped all of the cum off of her. His long pink dick had grown and was peeking out at the waiting perfect ass.

"Come on boy, get her! Get her boy!" shouted Black as he helped Bruno up and onto Tiffany. Bruno started humping her as soon as he rose up on two legs.

"That's it boy. Fuck that ass. Fuck it boy!!"

Brigette was no longer in the dark as to what was going down. She shook her head. She wanted to cry for her friend. But the tears wouldn't fall.

She hung up the phone and pulled a suitcase from under her bed. It was time. It had been four years. They say that you have to clean up where you fucked up. Her friend was in trouble. It was time to go home.

An hour later she was at Rochester's Greyhound Bus station. She'd spent all of the money that she had. She purchased a one-way ticket, to Niagara Falls, New York,

Back at Tiffany's...

The men had finished making their video.

"I can sell a few copies of this to get our money back," said Black holding the cartridge up in the air.

"Cut her sorry ass loose," he ordered.

Cleve pulled out a ridged hunting knife and cut all of Tiffany's restraints off. She lay motionless across the over-turned chair.

"Get up bitch. We're letting you live today." Black kicked her in the ass. Tiffany fell to the floor. Her eyes were wide open and she lay completely still.

Cleve put his hand in front of her nose. She wasn't breathing. He pulled the sock out of her mouth. Her throat fought to release it.

"Damn man, she must have swallowed the sock. She choked on the goddamn sock." Cleve dropped the sock.

"Let's get the fuck out of here," shouted T-Bone.

All of them started running down the stairs. Bruno was running with them...

• • •

I had taken the fare home and was on my way home when I looked down at the floor. It looked like several balled up plastic bags. I leaned over and picked it up. One bag contained several blocks of crack. Flakes fell from the outside bag. I brushed off the flakes and smelled my hand. It smelled like old pussy.

It wasn't hard to figure out what had happened. Good old Tiffany had tricked with the three gentlemen, then stole their dope. They found out that their shit was missing as soon as she'd bounced. That's why they were after her. The devious bitch.

I stuffed the package into my pocket and drove home. Nae Nae and Jessica were sitting in the middle of the bed watching TV.

"Daddy, daddy!" screamed little Jessica as she ran to the edge of the bed and jumped up into my arms. I remembered back when Tatiana was her age right before her mother ran out on us.

"Chris, what's the matter? You look spaced," asked Nae Nae as she took Jessica from me and laid her back down.

"Nothing. Nothing at all," I lied as I pulled Nae Nae close to me. We kissed a long deep, love-filled kiss. I undressed and hopped in bed. Nae Nae tucked under my arm, between me and my child waiting for the child to go to sleep.

Chapter Nine

Brigette glanced at her watch as the Greyhound bus pulled up into the Buffalo bus station. It was 1:35 AM. "Damnit!" She had just remembered that the last metro to leave Buffalo headed toward the Falls had left out at 6:22.

She got her suitcase and took a seat near door 16, the one reserved for the 40 metro. She curled up in the seat and fell asleep. At 8:00 AM she was awakened by the need to relieve herself.

Coming out of the restroom she saw several people sliding coins into various vending machines for a variety of goodies. She reached into her pocket and pulled out 17 cents, all of the money she had to her name. She needed $1.25 to get to the Falls. She thought to herself, *Now what the fuck do you do?* She went outside. To the left was the taxi stand. It cost $35.00 to get to the Falls by cab, so that was out.

To the right were an all night restaurant and a couple of hotels. Naw, they meant trouble.

She pulled out her cell phone and called Tiffany. All she got was a busy signal. She went back inside to where she had left her suitcase. But it was gone. She ran all over the station looking, but it was not to be found. She plopped down in the seat closest to her and cried.

She picked up her cell phone and called Chris. Nae Nae answered, still glowing after a heated lovemaking session.

"Hello? Hello?"

Brigette didn't answer. Instead she quickly hung up checking to see how much power remained. She saw that there were only two bars left.

Feeling helpless, she started to walk. She had no idea where she was going. She just walked. Different street names flashed before her. None seemed familiar. She'd been to Buffalo many times, but that was out near Jefferson and Bailey. Never was she downtown on foot. An hour later she was standing in front of McDonalds on Niagara Avenue. The smell of fresh grilled burgers made her stomach ache of hunger. She walked up and looked into the large pristine window.

Six senior citizens sat in a corner area, drinking coffee, reading the Buffalo News and chatting up a storm. A LaSalle taxi out of Niagara Falls pulled up. Two young Black men hopped out and ran inside of the McDonalds heading straight toward the restrooms.

Brigette's feet were starting to hurt. She sat down at one of the six outside tables. Minutes later the two young black men came out of McDonalds, drinking coffee and carrying two bags of food.

Her eyes followed the young men all the way to the taxi. As soon as they opened the door to get in, she jumped up and ran over to them.

"Hey! Hey guys!!" she yelled.

Both men stopped, eyeing the fine assed snowflake that was running toward them. The short, fat coal-black one with bad teeth spoke back.

"Yo, baby girl. How can we be of service?"

His breath reeked of alcohol and cigarettes. A large gold cross hung from his neck. He wore a tan and white Gucci sweatsuit with white Airforce One sneakers. The waves in his hair were deep and formed full circles around his head.

The other man wore an all white Louis Vuitton velour outfit. He too wore tight waves in his head but he had a friendly smile and a nice set of teeth.

"Hey guys, are you headed back to the Falls?'

"And if we are?" asked the one with the bad grill.

Brigette shuffled her feet and looked down at the ground. Unconsciously, when she put both hands behind her back, she pushed her chest up forcing her breasts up and out.

Both men gawked at her. Neither her pink sweater, nor her loose-fitting, knee length skirt could hide her tight-assed body.

"Yes miss lady, we're headed back to the Falls," answered the one with the nice smile.

"I'm sorta stuck here in Buffalo. I left Rochester last night headed toward the Falls to see a friend. I went to the rest-room, and when I got back my luggage was gone. So I'm stuck...unless you can see it in your hearts to let me catch a ride with you."

"What's in it for us?" answered the short fat one.

"Look, you've got me all wrong. All I need is a ride. I can pay you once I catch up with my friend."

She looked into the tall one's eyes. He smiled. His teeth glistened in the sun.

"OK, Get in."

The short one jumped in first forcing Brigette to sit in between them. The turban wearing, bearded driver leered at them in the rear view mirror. Large yellow teeth separated his lips.

"Yo, snowflake, what's your name? You look familiar. Have you ever been in the Falls before?" He leaned over almost on top of her. He pawed at the hem on her skirt. "I'm sure that we've met somewhere before."

"No, I don't think so. I'm sure that we've *never* met." She removed his hand from her skirt.

The driver flew up Niagara Avenue and turned onto I-190 headed for the falls. His eyes were still glued to his rear view mirror.

"Kenny, be cool man. We're just giving the lady a ride. Leave her be!"

Kenny sat back in his seat fuming. "Look man, I'm telling you that I've seen this ho somewhere before. I know it."

Anthony, the nicer of the two turned and started to stare out of the window. *Shopping.*

The roar of the engine, the silence, the comfort of the seat combined, lulled Brigette to sleep. Twenty minutes later, they rolled up in the parking lot of the Casino Seneca.

Brigette felt someone gently nudging her.

"Hey, little momma. Wake up. We're here in the Falls. Brigette raised her head up off of his shoulder. She'd fallen over onto his shoulder during the ride. Her skirt had risen up her healthy thighs. She tugged at her skirt as she struggled to sit upright. Anthony opened the door and stepped out. Reaching down he helped Brigette out. Kenny reached out pretending to squeeze her ass, and then slid out behind her.

"Thanks for the ride. Do you have a number that I can call, so that I can pay you when I get the money?"

Anthony pulled out a business card. It read "Tony's Furniture Store."

"OK Tony. I'll call you some time tomorrow. Thanks again for the ride." She shook both men's hands and took off up Niagara Street to find Tiffany. Standing on the corner of Tenth and Niagara were two young white strawberries. She walked to them.

"Hey, either of you girls know Tiffany?"

Both girls looked at each other and giggled.

"It is so."

"It is not."

"I'm telling you, it is her."

The freckle-faced red head asked, "Is your name Strawberry?"

A deep red flush exploded across Brigette's face. How could these young crackheads possibly know who she was? She cleared her throat and answered. "No, why, no, it's not," she lied."Now, do either of you girls know a ho named Tiffany. She's been out here for years."

"I told you it's not her. She was prettier."

"OK, OK, so you were right," said the blonde.

"Tiffany lives up the block, six houses down, upstairs.'

"Thank you. You girls be careful." As Brigette left the girls, she could hear them still debating.

"I still swear that's her. I don't know why she's lying, but that's her.'

Brigette walked down six houses and went to the side door. She pushed it open and went to the third floor. The door was partly opened.

"Tiffany! Tiffany, are you here?"

Brigette pushed the door wide open. It bumped something on the other side of it.

"AAAgghh!" she screamed at the top of her voice.

There, on the other side of the door lay a naked and dead Tiffany. Brigette ran down the stairs and out to the street wondering where to go next.

Chapter Ten

She ran to the halfway house on Memorial Parkway where she explained all that she knew to the counselor on duty. The counselor called the police. The Medical Examiner ruled the death was the result of suffocation. They also found semen in her rectum and dog's semen in her vagina.

All of the sordid details were plastered in the Niagara Gazette. Brigette was given a room in the community missions building. She ate at the soup kitchen. They also gave her a voucher for clothes from the Goodwill.

She walked over to Ontario Avenue and picked up several articles of clothing. On the way back to the mission, she was approached by four well-dressed men.

"Well, well, well, if it ain't the hottest piece of ass in the city. What's up Strawberry?" said a stocky brown-skinned man with his hair French braided straight back.

"Girl, come give your boy a big hug."

Brigette looked over at the eye glass wearing young dark-skinned man.

"Cobbs! I thought you were in jail. When'd you get out?" asked Brigette.

"Me and Rice got out a couple months ago. Ced and Scott only did thirty months. Now, where have *you* been, sweetheart? I ain't seen you in a couple years."

"I've been out of town. Cleaning up my act."

"Naw, don't tell me that you've become one of those *N.A.* people."

"No, actually I'm one of those *A.A.* people. I started going to A.A. with Chris, my baby's daddy before I left, and it kinda stuck on me."

"No shit!" said Scott as he eyed Brigette up and down. She'd put on a few pounds in all the right places.

"Damn girl, we just came up big too, and the shot is blazing!" Cedric pulled five big slabs out of his pocket and flashed them in Brigette's face.

An old familiar feeling began to grow inside of her. At first there was a light stirring in the pit of her stomach. Then, slowly, an ever increasing warmth soon spread all over her body. She quickly said the Serenity Prayer. "God, grant me the serenity, to accept the things I can not change, the courage to change the things I can, and the wisdom to know the difference," then turned to walk away.

"Strawberry, wait!" Cobbs called out to her.

She froze. "Please, God, help me to walk away.'

"Strawberry, here's my number. I've got a car wash on Pierce Avenue. Call me if I can be of service." Cobbs handed her his business card, and she turned and walked away, sticking the card in her pocket.

She continued her journey, heading home. She walked past Tops, on Portage, seeing what seemed like dozens of familiar faces. She thought back to the girls on Tenth Street. The ones that told her where Tiffany lived. They seemed so familiar. Then somehow she remembered them. *Amber, the freckle-faced redhead, and Ashley, the blonde. But there was another one. One with raven black hair. Umm! Lisa! That's the other one's name. Lisa.*

A long white Lincoln stretch limousine approached her. Her breathing stopped until it passed. "Whew," she sighed.

It wasn't Chris. Brigette walked the rest of the way as fast as she possibly could.

Once she was safe back in her room, she lay on top of her bed contemplating how and when she was going to meet up with Chris and Tatiana. Soon she was fast asleep.

Meanwhile at the Patch...

Five young ladies came walking up Whirlpool Avenue having just crossed the Whirlpool Bridge from Canada. Kim was a short bouncy, blue-eyed, curly-haired blonde with nice round breasts. Summer was a dirty blonde, huge breasted, flat assed, tall girl. Teri was a cute well proportioned brunette. Patsy was a tall, wide-hipped, heavily made up black-haired Indian, and Tara was a tall gorgeous, stacked mulatto.

"He said that him and his buddies would meet us on the corner of Main and Ontario," said Kim as they trudged up the steep street of Whirlpool heading for Main.

"Well I hope that they show up. My feet hurt," complained Summer.

"Bitch, your pussy ought'a hurt. How could you let all four of them fuck you? We'd just met them." Tara was disappointed in Summer. She'd gotten drunk and fucked all of the boys that they'd just met and didn't get a penny for it. Now they were coming over to meet the guys again. Only this time it was business. *Money* business.

The girls walked over to Main and Ontario. They waited for two hours before the guys showed up.

"Black, what took you so long? We were just about to leave," Kim lied.

"Yeah, I could have danced at the Downer last night," chipped in Tara, meaning the Sundown, a popular Canadian Strip Club.

"I want to see some green before I go anywhere with anybody," protested Teri.

Black reached into his pocket and pulled out over four thousand dollars which he flashed at the ladies.

"Are you bitches with me?" he asked.

And like the Pied Piper of Hamlet who led the mice into the river, Black played them a tune of good sounding promises of drugs, money and fun.

They followed him back to an apartment that they used for business and tricking. They followed him up three flights of stairs and waited for him to unlock the door and lead them in.

The apartment was nicely furnished. Two leather sofas, a chaise lounge, and a love seat were made of expensive Italian leather. Two 40-inch flat screen televisions that showed two different porn videos and a Hitachi surround sound system that was plugged into one of the porn movies sat against a wall. Sounds of ecstasy filled the room.

"Yo fellows, we're here!" yelled Black.

Cleve, a slim light-skinned, glasses wearing, soft looking nigga stepped out followed by T-Bone and Stu, two dark-complexioned tough looking thugs. T-Bone wore tight waves in his hair and Stu sported a wild high, old school fro.

"Where's Steve?" asked Stu. "He should have been here with the shit by now."

Black pulled out his cell phone and called Steve. "Where the fuck are you, man? The hoes are here and we're ready to get this party started."

Steve burst out laughing. Everything always made Steve laugh. "I'm coming up the fuckin' stairs right this minute.' He stopped to catch his breath. He yelled into his phone, "Nigga, why can't you live someplace with an elevator? By the time I make it up these fucking stairs I'm going to be too tired to fuck." Steve burst into another laughing spasm.

"Hurry up, Blackman. Hurry up." Black closed his cell phone and dropped it on the sofa.

"I think that all of us have too many damn clothes on. Come one now, what ya'll think?" said Cleve as he started pulling his wife beater up and over his head. Several tattoos adorned his flabby body.

"I ain't taking off shit until I got some money," bitched Kim.

"If I don't get some money soon, I'm out of here. I could still make it to the Downer."

"Hell, I'm with you, Tara." offered Teri.

Suddenly the door burst open and Steve stumbled in. "Ta'daaa," sang Stave as he fell on to the floor.

"Steve, are you ever serious?" said Black as he stared down at his friend who was still lying on the floor. Black handed him five crisp one hundred dollar bills.

"This should at least be enough to get us started and there's plenty more where that came from if you girls are as good as you say you are."

"Alright. Let's party!" yelled Steve as he set out an ounce of powdered cocaine and several rolled up blunts of Canadian sticky icky.

The girls started taking off their clothes as they snorted and smoked all that they wanted. The men stuck to drinking the Hennessey.

An hour later, all of the women were naked and out cold sprawled all over the leather furniture. Black came out of the back bedroom holding a camcorder that was already recording.

"Cleve, get my money out of these bitche's pockets. T-Bone and Stu, carry these hoes into the bedroom. Steve, go get Bruno. We've got a movie to make."

"*Steve, go get Bruno.* Why do *I* always have to get Bruno? Do I look like I should handle the dog? Is that it? Do I look like a dog? If I do, then use *me*. We don't need Bruno. I'll fuck all of these bitches. You got some "E", some Viagra? Give me some Viagra, fuck Bruno."

Steve bitched all the way downstairs and out the back door. There, tied to a large tree, was a huge brown and white pit bull with an enormous head. Steve untied the dog and led him back into the building. He leaned over and patted the dog's huge head. "Come on Bruno, you've got work to do."

Chapter Eleven

Patsy slowly opened her eyes. She was on the cold concrete floor of some old dilapidated garage. Sunlight burst through several cracks in the flooring. She turned and froze as a burning sensation rocked through her side. Her fingers gently rolled across the scratches on her side, crossing her ribs.

"What the fuck? What the fuck did those bastards do to me?" she cried.

Teri, Tara, Summer and Kimberly began to stir. Kimberly's hands were rummaging through her pants pockets. Frantically, her nimble fingers ran in and out of every one of her pockets and each pocket came up empty.

"Dammit! Goddammit!"

"Fuck! What did those bastards give us?" asked Tara as she struggled to get to her feet. She winced and also found scratches on her side.

"They drugged us. They must have put something in with the coke. We snorted up their coke," said Patsy.

"Fuck that, I'm getting my money! These motha'fuckas ain't getting away with this shit. No fuckin' way." Patsy was upset. She covered her face with her hands and cried.

Tara was now on her feet. She looked through a broken window. "Where are we?"

"Does it matter? They got us. They got us good," said a very pissed off Kimberly.

Patsy finally made it to her feet and was headed toward the door. "I'm going back over there. I'm going to get my money. They don't know who the fuck they fuckin' with."

"So what 'chu gon' do? Go over there and talk your money out of them?" Kim was angry, but she was trying to be real about the situation.

"Well what are we supposed to do, Kim? Nothing?"

"No Patsy, we're going to do something alright, but let's be smart about it. They obviously had things planned for us. Let's return the favor."

"Mothafuckin' bastards. Count me in. I want those bastards for what they did to us. And what the fuck caused these scratches on my sides?" said Tara as she raised her blouse revealing four long parallel scratches on both her sides.

"Me too, I've got them on me too!" cried Teri.

"We've all got them. And I think I know where they came from. I've had them once before." Summer had all of the girl's attention, eager to learn what sadistic thing had been done to them to cause scratches that all five of them were inflicted with.

Patsy walked over and stood directly in front of Summer. She looked straight into her eyes. "OK, let's have it. What caused the scratches?" she asked.

"Are you sure you want to know?"

"Stop fuckin' around and tell us Summer. What the fuck caused the scratches?"

"Well, last year I went to this snowflake party and I got real drunk. The guy that I was with took me to his house and fucked the shit out of me. I fell asleep naked and wide legged. I was awakened by a tongue lapping at my cum-soaked pussy. I thought it was him, Roc, but it wasn't. It was his pit bull

Hammer. I was still horny and the dog's tongue felt so good that I bent over on all fours. I was drunk, horny and curious. Hammer hopped right up on the bed and mounted me. He acted like he'd done it before. He sure felt like he had.

"I was cumming for the third time when I heard Roc coming back into the room. I'd thought that he went to work. I tried to get loose from Hammer but couldn't. His little legs were wrapped tight around my waist. Roc came in and caught us. *Me, and his dog.* When Hammer finally let go, I had scratches…just like these. Scratches from his paws holding on to me."

"Dog Paws!! Dog paws!!" Patsy was shaking her head in disbelief as she spoke. "You mean that they drugged us so that we could get fucked by a fuckin' dog!!!"

Summer didn't answer. She didn't have to; there was no other explanation available.

"That's it! I'm going back to find those niggas. I'm gon' find my girl, Sheka. She can get me a gun. I'm gon' get me a gun and kill those niggas. I'm gon' get them for what they did to us. I'm gon' get them!" Tara's body shook. Tears were pouring down her face, and her voice quivered as she spoke.

A loud voice came through the window. "Hey, what are you girls doing in my garage? Get out of there."

A light-skinned, bald headed man was peering through the broken window. He smiled showing off pink gums where his front teeth should have been. The girls opened the side door of the garage and ran out. The bald, toothless man was standing there, mouth opened smiling.

"You ladies got sumptin' to smoke, some rock, some Flav, some get high?"

The smile on his face seemed to be plastered there. Even when he spoke he seemed to be smiling.

"No, we don't have no crack. Now leave us alone," said Patsy. "Get away from us."

"Stokes don't bother nobody. Stokes min' his own business. Y'all in Stoke's house. Stokes don't bother nobody." He talked in the third person which the girls found amusing. In the last few hours it was the only thing that the girls had to smile about.

Stokes reached behind him and pulled his shopping cart full of bottles and cans in front of him. Then he pushed it inside of the now empty garage.

Stokes stood next to Tara, who was the tallest of the girls and looked down at her bulging breast. Tara turned her back to the man which made him smile even more as he gazed at her ample behind. "I'm outta here. I'm going to find Sheka. Y'all with me or what?"

"Not me. I've been through enough shit. Fuck this country! Fuck a nigga! And fuck y'all for getting me into this shit!" screamed a crying Kimberly.

"Me too. I just want to go home and forget that this shit ever happened," said the whorish Summer.

Patsy, Tara and Teri headed toward 24th and Niagara Street, the old Strawberry Patch. But the streets were empty. No hoes. No dealers. No slow rolling cars.

They walked over to 24th and Cudabeck. On the corner of Cudabeck was a brown and white two-family house. They walked up on the porch and rang the buzzer to the downstairs apartment.

A short redbone girl with blondish hair answered,"Yes, may I help you?" The redbone was wearing a long red sheer nightgown. Everything that she had was there to be seen-tits, ass, everything.

"New York, who's at the door?" A taller, big butt girl walked from the rear of the house. All she wore was a short white slip. "Sheka wants to know who's at the fucking door."

"Tara. Tell Sheka that Tara wants to see her. It's important."

The big butt girl ogled at Tara's fine ass. "I'll bet it is important, honey," she mumbled as she turned and walked away.

Seconds later she returned. "Sheka says to have a seat. She'll be right with you."

Patsy, Tara and Teri sat on the white brocade sofa. They looked around the expensively furnished room. Five minutes had passed and they were still sitting there. Patsy jumped up. "Fuck this shit. She knows we are waiting. Who the fuck do she think she is!" Patsy ran toward the back of the apartment. New York and the other girl named Detroit ran after her followed by Tara and Teri.

Patsy burst open the door to Sheka's bedroom. Sheka didn't stop what she was doing. A petite white girl with blonde hair had her legs spread wide as Sheka gave her the tongue lashing of her young life.

The young white girl barely looked sixteen. "Oh God! Yes Sheka, yes, yes, yes!" The girl began to shake all over as her body succumbed to a violent orgasm.

"What the fuck do you bitches waa.." Sheka's mouth dropped as she turned and faced the unexpected entourage of people.

Jumping out of the bed naked, she ran over and threw her arms around Tara's neck. "Tara, it is you." She stepped back and admired Tara's long, tall, well-proportioned body, showing no signs whatsoever of embarrassment.

"Damn Tara, you look good enough to eat."

"Sheka, all females look good enough to eat to you."

"Naw bitch, That big tit ho that was with you last year didn't. That was one nasty looking ho."

Patsy and Teri faced each other and screamed out, "Summer!"

"Yeah, that's that ho's name."

The young naked white girl got up, put on a terry cloth bath robe and helped Sheka put one on too.

Sheka led every one back to the living room. Sheka sat in a high back queen's chair. The white girl sat on the floor and laid her head against Sheka's leg. New York and Detroit sat on either side of them. Sheka had come up. She'd come up good.

"OK Tara. How can we be of service?"

"Sheka, we need a gun."

"Whoa, whoa girl. Guns bring trouble. Do you really need a gun?"

"Yes we do. We've got a score to settle," said a frustrated Patsy.

"It's a long story Sheka. But we really do need a gun," Tara pleaded.

"Well, then. We're all here, and I have plenty of time," said Sheka as she began to stroke the long blonde hair of the young white girl.

Tara began at the beginning, explaining their dilemma.

Chapter Twelve

Brigette was walking up 10th Street. She didn't really know where she was going, but she *did* know who she was looking for. She needed money. She needed a charger for her cell phone. She wanted some nice underwear, a McDonald's hamburger, and ice cream from Dairy Queen. Simple things. Things that she got clean to enjoy.

She found herself standing on the corner of 10th and Falls Street, pondering if she should turn a trick. Old behavior leads to relapse. This she had learned in the treatment center in Rochester, New York.

It was six o'clock in the morning. Where could she go? She was beginning to lose her mind, staying cooped up at the community missions. She needed to breathe. She walked on up Falls Street. Her experienced eyes searched deep inside of every car that would pass her by.

A black Chevy Monte Carlo slowed almost to a stop. Her heart raced. *Was this a trick?* Should she take it?

The car pulled off answering her questions for her. A beat up old Ford pickup pulled up beside her. Two young white men were in it. One of them called out to her. "Yo baby, wanna come and party with me and my man Josh?"

Brigette kept walking, trying to ignore them. She was hoping that they'd pull away. They weren't looking to trick.

They were looking for a freebie. A fuck for a few drinks and cigarettes.

She remembered the times past when the streets were hot and she needed a place to go, when she'd taken a few horny men up on offers such as the previous one. She'd done it just to get off the streets.

But today, this wasn't the case. She had a place to go to. So she walked. Her legs became weary. *Funny ain't it,* she thought, *I used to walk in circles for hours chasing that rock. And I've only been walking abut forty-five minutes now. I need to rest.*

She remembered that there was a park bench over on Buffalo Avenue and 24th. She headed across 24th Street.

Sheka and Amanda, Sheka's young white blonde friend, stepped out on to their front porch. New York and Detroit were still out tricking. A red Cadillac Escalade pulled in front of her house. The tinted passenger window eased down.

"Sheka! What's up baby girl?"

Sheka came down from the porch and walked over to the open window. "What's up Ced? Cobbs? Scott?" She nodded as she recognized each individual sitting inside of the plush truck. They each nodded back at her.

"Where's New York?" asked Cobbs. His eyes lit up with anticipation.

"She's not here at the moment. But I'll tell her that you asked about her."

Scott leaned over and stuck his whole head out the window and said, "Damn Sheka, when you gonna let me get a slice of your little chump there?" referring to little Amanda

Amanda blushed and stepped behind Sheka.

"She's my private toy. She ain't on the market yet."

"So what 'chu sayin'? Our money ain't green enough? Our dope ain't Flav enough? Or is it that she don't do big black dicks?"

Sheka knew what game Ced was playing. No white girl could survive in the hood if the word got out that she was prejudiced. Not even under *her* wing.

She put her arm around Amanda and grabbed a handful of her tiny tight ass. "Give me another week or so, to break things in properly."

The fellas laughed.

Sheka stared at the white girl heading in their direction. The fellas turned to see what she was staring at so intently. The white girl had a familiar aura about her. They all turned to watch as the figure drew closer.

"That *is* her."

"Naw, she's too tall."

"She is not, too tall. That's her I tell you."

"Bet fifty it ain't her.'

"Bet."

"Let me outta here," said Scott as he opened his door and stepped out. "Yo! Strawberry!!" he shouted as he started walking in her direction.

Brigette heard her name being called, but she wasn't sure who it was that was calling her. Her feet were starting to burn. Her eyes were fixated on the two figures standing on the porch. The black girl looked like…maybe...Sheka?

Sheka started down the stairs, fully recognizing her long lost friend.

Both girls ran toward each other, meeting and embracing in the middle of the street. Sheka easily lifted Brigette into the air. They kissed. A deep long kiss.

Amanda dropped her eyes to the floor of the porch. Jealousy began to boil inside her.

"Pay up Nigga," Scott said to Cobbs.

"Yeah, there's only been one bitch in the whole city that can make Sheka jump. That's her, strawberry." Cedric killed the motor to the Escalade and stepped out.

Amanda ran back in the house. She'd heard Sheka talk of this bitch, Strawberry, and she had no desire to meet her.

"Damn Strawberry, you look good enough to eat." Sheka's lame line still had its effects.

"And when I need to be eaten there's nobody else in the world that I'd like to eat me, but you Sheka. Damn girl. I've got so fuckin' much to tell you. Can we go inside and talk?'

Their embrace ended and Sheka grabbed her hand, leading Brigette back to her house. Looking up at the porch Sheka noticed that Amanda was no longer standing there.

"Shit!" she cursed louder than she wanted to.

"What's the matter?" asked Brigette as she quickened her pace to keep up with the almost running Sheka.

"Nothing. Nothing that can't be fixed."

As they approached the Escalade, the boys started to fuck with Brigette.

"Damn Strawberry, what's up with those clothes? You need me to take you to Lerner's or something. It'll be worth it to spend a little with you." Cobbs pulled out a wad of green and flashed it.

Sheka pushed past the three fellas, knocking Cobb's knot out of his hands. Money went everywhere.

"She don't need shit from you, Cobbs. And I do mean that literally! She's with me now!!"

"Fuck you Sheka!! You too Strawberry! Fucking dikes!!!"

Sheka smiled and exaggerated her hip movement as they passed the wanna be gangsters. She slapped Strawberry on the ass, leaving her widespread hand on her butt, pulling her up the stairs and onto the porch.

Seconds later they vanished inside of the house.

Cedric got back into the Escalade followed by his two henchmen. "Fuck them hoes for now. Rice is waiting for us. Sooner or later those bitches will be begging for us. They always do."

Sheka watched out the window as the truck pulled away. Smiling, she pulled Bridgette into her lap. "Amanda!! Get out here! We've got company!"

Chapter Thirteen

Patsy and Tara were sitting inside Frankie's all night restaurant, waiting for Teri. They needed a gun and were out doing what they had to do in order to get one.

They drank coffee and smoked cigarettes for over an hour when Teri and two heavyset men stepped in and joined Patsy and Teri at their booth. Patsy gave Teri a questioning look. "What's up?" she asked.

"This is Kenny," she said pointing to one. "And this is Anthony." She pointed to the other. "They have something that you guys need to hear."

"Teri, it's late and we've been out all night. Can't the shit wait," Patsy pushed her coffee away from in front of her.

"Chill sexy momma. This will definitely interest you," said Kenny as he put his hand on top of Patsy's.

"OK, spill it. I've got things to do."

"Chill momma." Kenny loved drama. He was eating the shit up. All eyes were on him. "Two nights ago, me and my man Anthony were at a snowflake party in Buffalo, you know, white girls galore."

That shit wasn't interesting to Patsy in the least. She rolled her eyes up in her head to let them know that she was ready to bounce. She stood up.

Kenny continued with his story. "We were all getting high and shit, when this guy sticks this video into the VCR. It had him and his crew three bangin' this white chick. You know what *three bangin'* is don't you? One in her pussy, one in her mouth and one in her ass.

"Well we start freakin' with two of the white hoes. We were changin' partners when a dog appeared in the video. A pit bull named Brutus."

"Bruno," Anthony corrected.

"Yeah Bruno. Well anyway, by now the girls in the movie are so high that they'll fuck anything. And that's just what they did. They even fucked the dog."

Patsy plopped back down in her seat. Listening.

"Well anyway, last night I see these scratches on Teri's side and I think to myself. *These are odd ass scratch marks on her flawless white body.* And I know that I've seen them some place before.

"Yeah, then I remember where I'd seen them. The video!! The dog left those kinds of scratch marks when they would pull him off of one chick to go fuck another." Anthony told Patsy what she needed to hear.

Summer was right. They'd all been fucked by a dog.

"Now me and my man Anthony, we done a lot of shit ourselves, but this shit ain't right."

"Right, me and my man Ken don't go along with raping women with dogs. That's too low."

Tears began to run down Tara's face. She made no attempt to hide them nor wipe them away.

"Then Teri said that she didn't remember anything about how she got her scratches. We thought that the girls in the video were just skee'd. But now we figure that they were drugged."

"The coke. They must have put something in the cocaine. The rotten bastards." Teri and Patsy both now had teary eyes.

"You know we've got a code in the hood that one Black man may never raise his hand against another over a white ho'." Anthony stood up and raised his balled fist high over head and slammed it hard against the table.

"But Teri told us that they did it to you too," he said facing Tara. "They fucked up there. They fucked up 'cause *you* are one of *us*. *You're Black!!"*

Tara wiped her tears away. "So you guys will help us?"

"That's why we're here," said Kenny.

"And what's in it for you?" asked Patsy always suspicious of people and there motives.

Kenny smiled and wiped saliva from the corners of his mouth. "You baby. All I want is you."

"So I fuck you and you run off and join your buddies that drugged us."

"You got me all wrong, momma. And those surely ain't no buddies of mine. Again, we came to help. There's probably a video out there of the dog fuckin' the shit out of you. We think that we can help you find it as well as help you get even with those punks."

"Come on Kenny, let's go. Fuck these hoes."

Both men rose to leave. Anthony lifted Tara's hand to his lips and kissed it. "It's been a pleasure to meet you." And they left.

"Well thanks, Patsy. I fucked the both of them all night long to get them here and you and your smart-assed mouth chases them off in a few minutes."

"All them niggas wanted was some pussy, girl. Wake the fuck up and smell the roses."

"So fucking what!! They get a little pussy, and we get some payback. Is that bad? We've been getting fucked ever since we started coming over here to the States. Is it wrong to at least try and get some get back?"

Teri's cries made sense. All of them had been fucked over many times before. They'd all had dreams of getting some payback. And now, she'd blown their chance.

Patsy put a ten dollar bill on the table and motioned to the others that it was time to leave.

They walked down Portage to Buffalo Avenue then crossed over to the Majestic Motel, a $24.99 a night modestly furnished spot. They slept in the same bed. They ate cold cuts and crackhead soups. In one night they'd accumulated two hundred dollars. After one more night, they should have enough to buy a piece.

The room was hot. The girls stripped down to their undies and piled on top of the bed. Tara fell right to sleep. Patsy and Teri lay next to each other, not being too careful about where bodies touched.

"Teri." She whispered "I'm sorry about what happened today. I realize that you'd gone through a lot to get those two to come and help us. I was rude. I'm sorry. Truly sorry."

Patsy reached out and stroked Teri's shoulder length hair. Without replying, Teri got up and went into the bathroom. Soon the water in the shower was turned on. Patsy got up, removed the remainder of her clothes and joined a waiting Teri in the steaming hot shower.

Chapter Fourteen

Sheka and Amanda waited patiently for Brigette to come out of the dressing room. Finally she came out wearing a turquoise, thin spandex pant suit. The weight she'd gained while in rehab was still there, in all the right places.

Her hips were now fitting the size 7/8 pants completely. Her breasts stretched the matching short sleeve top to maximum perfection.

Brigette spun around full circle, shaking her ass as she did, modeling for her two friends.

"You look scrumptious, baby girl. Simply scrumptious."

"Yeah, I have to admit. Eh! You do look great," added Amanda.

Brigette admired herself in the mirror. "Are you sure I don't look fat?" she asked.

"No baby, you look perfect. Definitely good enough to eat!"

"My God! Haven't you done enough of that this morning?"

"We can never get enough of your sweet pussy. Do we baby?"

Amanda blushed and nodded her head up and down. Sheka handed her platinum Visa card to the store clerk. "We'll take it. She'll wear it out. And the white sandals too."

The clerk added the items. "That'll be $136.00 plus tax."

"A hundred and thirty-six dollars!! No way!! That's too much money!!!" shrieked Brigette.

"It's my money and I want you to have it," barked Sheka.

"Sheka likes to buy things for us. She buys me things all the time. Don't dis her by refusing her gift. Take it." pleaded Amanda.

Brigette sat down and put the white sandals on that went with her turquoise outfit. They felt good on her feet. They looked perfect.

By the time the girls got home, New York and Detroit were there sitting on the sofa. A shower was running in the background.

Puzzled, Sheka asked, "Who's in the shower?"

"We knocked off a new one. Nineteen years old. Half and half, with an ass that'll stretch from New York to Detroit. At least it did this morning." They burst out laughing.

"At least it did this morning, bitch, y'all crazy," said Brigette.

"What's the bitch's name?" asked Sheka.

"Chicago. We named her Chicago. Wait 'til you see her. She's F.I.N.E." New York was proud of what she'd done. She knew that Sheka was extremely selective on who she allowed to stay in her place. They knew that Chicago had better be that girl. Sheka walked straight to the bathroom and walked right in. She didn't believe in knocking on doors in her own house. She threw the shower curtain back.

Chicago had her back to Sheka, rinsing the shampoo from her curly black hair. Slowly she turned, letting the steamy hot water run down her voluptuous body as if she knew that Sheka was watching. She definitely had more ass than Sheka was accustomed to, but it was all well put together.

Chicago turned the water off.

Sheka handed her a towel.

Chicago slowly dried herself. Seductively, she dried herself. When she was done, she handed the damp towel back to Sheka and stepped out of the tub.

"You must be Sheka. How are you? I've heard so much about you." She spoke then continued on in to the spare bedroom.

Sheka had to admit, the new girl Chicago was hot, beautiful *and* confident. She liked confidence in her women.

She raised the towel up to her nose and inhaled deeply. She took in the full aroma of Chicago's scent. Then she tossed the towel to the floor and went into the spare bedroom.

Chapter Fifteen

Black, T-Bone and Cleve had just come back from being served. They were discussing how to place the six bricks that they'd come up with.

"Black, Cedric and them niggas want a brick a week now. They doin' alright with the shit. I been frontin' it for $25,000 and they've been payin' me in four days," bragged Cleve.

"Good, then they should be able to pay cash for what they need. No more frontin'."

"Damn Black, I just started frontin' these to Heavie over on Falls Street. They just moved up to 250 grams. The money's good, but they ain't got no real bank. They can't afford no cash," complained T-Bone.

Neither man wanted any parts of the cash *only* business. Both men were skimming money off of the man that they fronted. Cash would only hurt them badly.

Suddenly the door opened to the bathroom that they were in. Steve came in puffing, followed by Bruno.

"That's it. That's the last time that I walk that damn dog. He tries to eat up everything that he sees, other dogs, cats, squirrels. Everythang. He even wanted to bite a little old white lady with a red and white cane for being blind. That's it! I'm done!!"

Bruno started barking. Everyone burst out laughing.

"Oh, so now I'm a clown, huh? I'm a clown now?"

Steve grabbed Cleve's light ass and hoisted him high in the air.

"Hey nigga, put me down before I whup your big ass!" Cleve was always wolfing about who his skinny ass could beat. The truth was, he was too light in the ass to beat anybody.

"Put him down Steve before you hurt his skinny ass."

It was more of a request than an order. But Steve let Cleve slide down onto the floor. Cleve turned a beet red as he hopped back up to his feet. Quickly he threw up his dukes and charged at Steve. T-Bone grabbed Bruno by the collar.

One, two, three. One, two, three. Cleve hit Steve with six lightning fast jabs. Steve laughed as he easily brushed off the mosquito like punches and charged Cleve as he danced around on the floor.

Steve hit Cleve once and the fight was over. Cleve lay on the floor, holding his jaw. Black ran over and pulled Steve up off of the much smaller, weaker man.

"Come on Steve, we don't need him hurt. I ain't payin' no hospital bill."

"Well he hit me first. Talk to *him*."

"I would if he could hear me, but you knocked him the fuck out."

T-Bone helped get Cleve to his feet. Cleve almost went down again. They half carried, half dragged him to the sofa. Cleve came to and started struggling with T-Bone and Black. They held him down so that he wouldn't hurt himself.

Steve was still complaining. "Ever since I first came in with you guys I've been the fall guy, the brunt of all your fucking jokes. Well it ends today. No more fall guy. NO more."

Steve sat on the sofa, still fuming. Cleve was wide awake now and other than a sore jaw he was alright.

"I'm sorry Cleve. It wasn't your fault. It's everything else man. I'm sorry." Steve extended his hand. Cleve hesitated to take it.

"Come on man, I said I'm sorry. Take my hand." Steve extended his hand further.

Cleve reached out, taking Steve's hand. Steve grabbed it and pulled Cleve up off the couch and into his powerful arms. He gave Cleve a playful hug.

"Put me down, nigga. See, you play too damn much."

Steve burst into one of his patented robust, belly-slapping laughs. "OK Cleve, just don't hit me no more."

Black went into the kitchen. "Come on men, We *are* men, aren't we?"

Everybody met in the kitchen. Even Bruno followed.

"OK, we'll give everybody sixty days notice that from then on it's cash and carry. Alright? That should be plenty enough time for them to get themselves together."

Everyone agreed.

"Cleve, you and T-Bone can help out with the chores. Steve's right. He's a crew member, not our whipping boy. You got that?"

T-Bone and Steve agreed.

"Now let's get down to business." The four men went about the business of cooking and distributing the crack.

T-Bone and Cleve went out to get more baking soda. While they were out, Cleve started scheming. "I'm gon' fuck Steve's ass up someday. Black ain't gon' be able to save his punk ass all the time. Who the fuck do he think he is? Knocking me out. I'm gonna fuck him up real good. You'll see. You'll see."

A tear fell from Cleve's eye. T-Bone saw it. It was a sign, letting him know that one day, for sure, Cleve was going to fulfill his promise.

The house phone rang. Black answered it. "Hello."

"What's up my nigga? It's me, Babybra!"

"Who?"

"It's me. Babybra, Nigga! Babybra!!"

"Babybra. Where the fuck are *you*? I heard that you was still up in Lewisburg doin' a dime piece."

"Naw Nigga, I only had to do five. I want to hook up. Rap a little. Know-ow-mean?"

"Straight. I'll call Cleve and have him pick you up. What's the address?'

"1266 Centercourt. I'm at my mom's house."

"Cool, Cleve's over that way anyhow. Be looking out for him."

"What's he driving?"

"My black Navigator.'

"On 24's."

"You know it."

"Damn! I can't wait to rap. Black rollin' in the black Navigator on 24's."

"OK Babybra, I'm out." Black hung up the phone and walked into the living room where Steve was playing with Bruno.

"Steve!"

"Yeah Black."

"You still seeing that chick that works at the police station?'

"Sherry? Sure, we still kick it every now and then.'

"Good. Have her check out a man named Stewart Gibson, birthdate March 23, 1980. Just got out of Lewisburg. Find out if he's clean or not?"

"How soon you need to know?"

"I'm about to call Cleve to pick him up.'

"That soon, huh."

"Yeah, *that* soon."

"OK, Black. I'm out." Steve got up from off of the floor and quietly left.

Black dialed Cleve's cell number. "Hello, Cleve?"

"This is he."

"Do you remember Babybra? Babybra Hodge?"

"Of course I do. Got hit with 10-15. Doing it up in Lewisburg."

"Correction. He's out. Just called me. Wants to come and rap."

"Sounds fishy to me, man."

"Yeah, I know. Pick him up and meet me at the place on Whitney. Me and Bruno should be there by the time that you get there...and Cleve,"

"Yeah."

"Let me do the talking, alright?"

"Don't I always, nigga."

Both men hung up. T-Bone grabbed the baking soda and stashed it in the back of the truck. Black called Cleve back.

"Don't you need his address?"

"He's probably staying at his mom's in Centercourt. I think it's 1266.'

"Great memory."

"It'll do."

Black hung up and put Bruno's leash on him. "Come on. I think I smell a rat."

Chapter Sixteen

Nae Nae was working for the county as a caseworker. She loved her job. It was the kind of job that she had worked for and studied hard to have.

She wasn't stuck at an office desk. She had the freedom to move around. To travel. And what she loved most of all, was the ability to stop and check in on the kids, Tatiana and Jessica.

Nae Nae had always felt an inner need to help people. To help her people, as she often called them, to become a better, stronger, more educated people.

This was one of those days when she decided to stop at the house and peek in on the kids. She whipped her black Nissan Maxima around a rusted Jeep Cherokee and came to a stop at the light on the corner of Main and Depot.

"Hey girl! Hey you! Nae Nae!" The voice came from a frail looking freckle-faced red head and a petite blonde. Nae Nae recognized the girls. Both of them frequented the soup kitchen that she sometimes volunteered at.

Amber and Ashley, two veteran crack hoes. Nae Nae pulled over to the curb. The girls ran up to her.

"Have you seen her?"

"Did you know she was here?"

"See who. Know that *who* was here?" asked a perplexed Nae Nae.

"That girl, Strawberry. She's here. In the Falls."

The name had barely escaped Amber's lips when a chill went up Nae Nae's spine.

Why did that bitch come back here? And even more so, *What did she want?* Well whatever she wanted, she wasn't going to get it.

After composing herself, she asked, "When did you see here? Where?"

A glowing Ashley answered her. "A couple days ago down in the patch."

"The patch?" *Well, she's still tricking. Chris won't have nothing to do with no crack smoking, dick chasing ho.*

What could she want? Why did she have to come back? No, No, No, No No! She was not going to cause problems in her household. None.

Ashley and Amber could see how upset Nae Nae had become. The very mention of the name Strawberry had brought tears to her eyes, wrinkles in her forehead and caused the veins to rise at her temples.

"Mrs. Daniels, can we borrow five dollars." asked Ashley. She was trying her best to sound serious as if she had every intention of paying it back.

"Sure!" said Nae Nae as she picked up her purse from the floor, between her legs. She'd learned long ago that that was the safest place to keep your purse when you're riding through the hood. She set the purse on the seat next to her and fumbled through it. No fives, no tens, two ones. Her fingers danced through the rubble. She searched but came up empty. Finally she peeled a crisp twenty-dollar bill out and even though it was against her better judgment, she handed it to them.

Ashley and Amber's eyes lit up like four car fires on a dark summer night.

"Girls, this conversation never took place, OK."

The girls shrugged their shoulders, as if to say, *Who the fuck cares*. "OK," they answered.

Nae Nae whipped back out into traffic almost running into a metro bus. She didn't even remember driving the rest of the way home. All she knew was that she was pulling up in her driveway.

She went straight up the stairs and into the kid's rooms. Jessica was asleep in her bed while Lisa was reading a Harry Potter book to Tatiana in her room. Nae Nae walked over and kissed the sleeping child then went into Tatiana's room to check on her. She walked over and kissed Tatiana too.

Lisa kept on reading acknowledging Nae Nae's presence with a brief smile. Nae Nae turned and walked out of the room. *Good,* she thought *they were safe*. She picked up the phone and called me.

"Hello."

"Hey baby! I was just thinking abut you. You must have been reading my mind."

"Chris, any woman can read your mind. Sex."

"Only with you baby. Only with you. So what's up baby? Want me to stop by for a quick one? How much time do you have?"

"Oh, I guess I have a little time," she nervously began to twirl the phone cord. "So what's new Chris? See any interesting people? Anybody worth talking about"

She was trying to be subtle but failed miserably at it.

Suspicion began to creep into my head. I replied, "No, but should I have?"

"No! I was just curious about your day. That's all"

"Nae Nae! Are you sure?"

The chord became unplugged. The line went dead. Nae Nae had twirled the chord too hard. She jumped up and ran over to plug the phone back in. Her slim fingers danced over the buttons dialing me back.

I walked out of the office and jumped into a black Lincoln Towncar. I pulled off heading home. Something was odd about that phone call, but I had no idea what.

The office phone rang over and over.

"Nubian Chariot Limousine Service, this is Freddy. How may we help you?"

"Hi Freddy, this is Nae Nae. Is Chris there?"

"No, He just left. Try him on his cell phone.'

"OK, If he comes back, ask him to call me."

"Will do, Mrs. Daniels."

"Bye." She quickly dialed my cell phone. The answering service came on. "Shit," she swore. She knew that I was on my way home. I'd sensed that she was keeping something from me. And I was coming home to find out what!

I rode up Main to Pine Avenue. The red light caught me. I turned on my blinker, waiting so that I could make a left turn.

Two attractive white girls were walking up Pine Avenue carrying arm loads of clothes. Both were on the small side, though one was smaller than the other. Both were blonde, and both were built quite nicely.

I stared as they walked closer and closer. The taller girl must have found something funny because she burst out laughing.

I sat straight up. That smile. Was that? I killed the radio and lowered the window. My ears strained, listening to the blonde's laughter.

She laughed again. This time they were at the corner ten feet from my car. My heart pounded. I wanted to call out to see if it was her.

The light changed, and the girls crossed the street. I just sat there. Several cars that were behind me started to blow there horns in anger.

The girls turned and saw me staring at their behinds. Amanda started to exaggerate her swagger followed by Brigette exaggerating hers.

More cars began to blow.

I hit the gas and peeled out leaving a long black line in the street. I looked over my left shoulder as I sped past the two laughing women.

For a split second our eyes locked. There was no doubt. It was her. Strawberry was back!!

I kept driving heading home.

A fit of anger began to swell inside of me. *"See any interesting people?"* I remembered what Nae Nae had said. *"Anybody worth talking about?"*

The anger inside continued to grow. She knew. She knew that Brigette was back. *But why didn't she tell me?* Brigette is Tatiana's mother, she should have told me.

My anger continued to swell. I was so engrossed with anger that I didn't see Brigette try to wave me back. I didn't hear her call my name. I didn't notice the next traffic light turn red. I went through the light at 35 miles per hour. A huge red truck from Thompson's Roofing hit me broadside.

The next thing that I remembered, I was coming to, lying in a hospital bed at Memorial Hospital. My head was foggy. I wiped my eyes. Standing in front of me were two figures. They were both fuzzy. I closed my eyes and rested. Soon I was fast asleep.

"Chris, Wake up Chris. It's me Nae Nae."

I slowly opened my eyes. The bright hospital lights hurt my eyes. "Nae Nae, she's here. Why didn't you tell me?"

"Shhh Chris. Not right now."

"No! You don't understand. She's here." I wiped my eyes again trying to focus. I could barely make out my wife. Someone was standing off to the side. She didn't wear white.

Not a doctor or nurse. I tried harder to focus, but I still couldn't make out who it was.

"Who's that with you Nae?"

"Someone that's been waiting for a long time to see you Chris."

The figure came closer. It stopped right in front of me. I still couldn't see clearly. A hand touched me. A familiar touch.

"Hello Chris. It's been a while."

That voice. I snatched my hand away as if I'd been bitten by a rattlesnake.

"Brigette!"

Chapter Seventeen

Tenth Street, the new Strawberry Patch. Rarely was there an hour when the street wasn't busy. Just as Lundy's Lane was the infamous strip for Strip Clubs in Niagara Falls, Ontario, Chippawa Street was known for its many bars and clubs, so had 10th Street become known for its cornucopia of whores.

Beautiful young white and Asian whores from Canada, and Black and Indian whores from neighboring states all came to Niagara Falls, the honeymoon capital of the world.

The casinos, the new convention center, the entire renovation of downtown and Third Street helped to contribute to the financial growth of the city. Niagara Falls was a city on the move.

Drugs began to pour into the city. Despite efforts on the city police and the border patrol, ecstasy and crystal meth came from across the border in every conceivable method. Girls as young as fourteen were used as mules. They'd stuff their vaginas with plastic bags filled with drugs. Toddler's toys were often packed with thousands of E pills. Dealers no longer had to go to Manhattan for cocaine. Local dealers had blown up so big, that the Buffalo, Syracuse and Rochester dealers were buying from them.

Canadian sticky icky from Vancouver was being shipped in by the tons. Chemical trucks were packed with 2-3 tons of plastic packed weed, and then filled with whatever product they were supposed to be hauling. Big trucks, tractor trailers and even small planes were used. But the majority of weed came across the border by boat, fishing boat. Hundreds of boats a day.

Rice and a young light-skinned friend had just docked a 24′ boat at Fort Niagara docks. A long black suburban backed a trailer down to the boat. They secured the boat and began to pull it out of the water.

The driver threw the truck in four wheel drive and stepped on the gas. The big engine bogged down under the strain of the weight of the huge boat. The big black tires began to grip. The boat finally cleared the water and crawled up to the top of the steep hill.

Rice and his friend jumped into the truck and they hit the Robert Moses Expressway. Twenty minutes later they pulled into the *Do It Yourself* car wash on 11th Street.

A blue pickup with a matching cab pulled up behind them. Two dread wearing Jamaicans got out and opened the cab. Rice climbed up on the boat and opened the door to the cuddy cabin.

Sitting on the floor on the cuddy was 100 kilos of prime fish scale cocaine. They unloaded the coke into the back of the pickup. It took less than twenty minutes.

"Take this shit to the spot. Rice'll be there in the morning to split it out," directed the bald man.

"Ya man, me going straight der, right now man." He pulled out a blunt that was packed so full of weed that some of it was dropping down to the ground.

"Hey, we don't get high on the job. Put that shit away."

"No man. Me don't put the gongi away. Gongi a natural man. Me always smoke gongi. Always man." He lit the blunt, inhaled and smiled.

"Rice, where'd you get this asshole? You know the rules."

"Calm down Geno. These are the best men in the city. They work hard, they don't fuck with the product and they keep their mouths shut."

"Rice! Fuck it. Let's get out of here." Geno and Rice got back into the Suburban and pulled up in front of Nubian Chariot Limousine Service. Geno opened the overhead doors and Rice pulled in next to the stretch Hummer.

Geno was still pissed at the reefer smoking Jamaican. "Rice, I don't like it when people are getting high while handling my merchandise."

"Geno, come on. They've been doing this for the last five years, and ain't nothing happened yet."

"Right, yet!! I ain't get back in this shit to get busted on a humble. Can't they wait 'til they get back to the spot?"

"OK, OK, I'll tell them to when I get back there in the morning. And Geno, I might have to lay low for awhile, Cedric is getting a little suspicious."

"Good. With Chris in the hospital, I'm going to be busy for a minute anyhow. See you in about ten days."

"Cool." Rice pulled the Suburban out. He flipped open his cell phone and called Cedric. "What's up Ced?'

"Same shit, different night. Where you at?"

"I'm up on the Patch, looking for some new shit."

Rice was cruising down Tenth Street. The patch was lit up like Christmas. Girls were everywhere. Cars were pulling over left and right. Window shopping was definitely going down.

"Damn!!! Ced, you should see what I'm looking at. Damn these bitches is hot."

"Well pick 'em up and bring 'em here, nigga! Bring 'em here!"

Rice pulled over and lowered the tinted window. "Yo! Snowflake!!!"

Two young white hoes walked over to the truck. "Hi, nice truck. What's on your agenda tonight?"

"Hopefully you are. Hop in."

Both girls climbed into the backseat of the big truck.

"What's your name, big boy?"

"They calls me Rice. What's yours?"

"Maria," answered the one with the huge tits and dark hair.

"And my name is Sarah," answered the slender built blonde. "Where are we going?" asked Sarah.

"Does it matter?"

"No, not really. As long as we get paid. I need a hit badly," said Maria, massaging her breasts and licking her lips.

Rice was staring into his rearview mirror.

"Yo, Maria! Are those things real?"

"What these?" she said as she raised up her blouse and bounced her huge breasts upside Rice's head.

"Goddamn baby, you're alright. I can see that we gon' have some fun tonight."

Rice pulled in front of Cedric's fuck house. This was where the fellows did all of their tricking. They got out and knocked on the door. Ced opened up.

"Damn Rice! All you ever pick up is white hoes. Ain't it any black ones out there?'

"Look, man. Look at how fine these bitches is!! You can even have first pick," argued Rice.

As soon as the door was closed, Maria grabbed the bottom of her blouse, pulled it up over her head and tossed it to Rice.

"Damn girl!! Are those real?" asked Cedric.

"Why don't you touch them and see?"

Smiling, Ced reached out and grabbed both bare breasts.

Chapter Eighteen

Chris had been in the hospital for six days. Each and every day, both Nae Nae and Brigette were there to see him.

Brigette had stopped at the information center and was on her way upstairs to room SW468. She pushed the button and waited for the elevator to come down from the sixth floor. It stopped at the fourth and second floors before finally arriving at the first.

An old white couple and two older black men with Bibles in their hands stepped off. Brigette went to step on when she heard her name being called.

"Brigette! Hold the elevator! Please wait!!"

Brigette turned and saw Nae Nae running toward her. She stepped inside the elevator and held the *door open* button.

Nae Nae ran into the elevator, breathing hard. She was trying to catch her breath. "Thank you. Thank you for waiting for me."

The elevator went up to the fourth floor. The door opened, and Brigette went to step out. Nae Nae stepped in front of her and pushed the button for the first floor. "I'm sorry. But we need to talk."

Brigette rolled her eyes up in her head and blew her breath hard. "What do we have to talk about?"

"About everything. About *my* man! *Our* children! About *our* lives and *your* presence. About everything, damn it."

"I don't see how any of this concerns me. I'm going up to see Chris."

Nae Nae stepped up in Brigette's face. "For what? What the fuck do you want? Money? Chris? If it's money you want, I'll give you what you want. If it's my husband that you want, well, you can't have him."

"I don't want your money. And Chris seems to be enjoying my company. We do have a child together."

"Then take your half breed brat and leave. Get the hell out of our lives!!" screamed Nae Nae.

The moment those words escaped her lips, she knew that she'd made a grave mistake.

"How long have you thought of Tatiana as a half breed brat? Does Chris know how you feel about her?"

Nae Nae didn't answer. She tried desperately to regain her composure.

The elevator stopped. The door opened. Two young black men entered. Both men ogled over the two attractive women. The door closed and the elevator began to move again.

"Yo! Snowflake! What's up?"

Strawberry nodded her head at the dark-skinned handsome young man. His hair was freshly cut and had the deep set waves in it. His teeth were pearly, which he proudly displayed with his ear to ear smile.

The other young man looked Nae Nae up and down but didn't say a word.

Nae Nae felt slighted. "What's wrong with young black men today? Do all of you have jungle fever or something? Is all y'all see are white women?"

She stood there hands on her hips waiting for an answer.

The guy that hit on Brigette spoke up first.

"Do you really want to know what's up?"

"I most certainly do!" she answered.

"Well, look at the shorts that she's wearing. Too tight and too short. Figure she's single and looking, might even be tricking."

He turned to Brigette and said, "No offense Miss."

"None taken," said a blushing Brigette.

The young man turned back to Nae Nae and continued his recitation.

"Now you, my beautiful black queen, are an entirely different story. Your clothes, your hair, your whole persona says money. High maintenance. That rock on your finger told me that you are married. Your voice and mannerisms were not of the ghetto. Out of our league so to speak."

"And you could tell all of that in the few seconds that you were in front of us?"

"You know it! Quicker if need be."

The young man jumped into the conversation. "You dig. If we looking for some real quick company then we gotta go for the snow. She's easier, not better, you dig."

Nae Nae started laughing. At first to herself and then loudly. The elevator stopped and the door opened. The level indicator pointed at the 4.

Both ladies stepped off.

"Well can a brother get a number?" yelled the second man.

Brigette and Nae Nae turned and walked away heading for Chris' room.

"Brigette?'

"Yeah!"

"Can we keep our conversation to ourselves?"

"For now, but we *are* far from finished."

"About Chris?"

"No, about my half breed brat."

They were standing in front of my room. They entered together showing no signs of indifference, at least none that I could see.

"Well good evening ladies. I'm glad that you two get along 'cause I think that Tatiana should see her mother." I struggled to sit up. I'd suffered three cracked ribs, a broken nose, and a mild concussion.

Brigette froze not knowing how she should respond to my request. Nae Nae slid beside me and helped me to a sitting position. "I think that's an excellent idea. Don't you Brigette?"

"I don't know. What's she going to think of me? I mean, I've been gone for so long. Do you think that she even remembers me?"

Brigette's stomach began to knot up. A familiar feeling began to grow inside of her. She closed her eyes and grabbed her stomach. She stayed like that for a moment. When she opened her eyes again, she found Nae Nae staring at her. Staring at her and smiling. She smiled because she knew. She knew that Brigette was fiening.

Chapter Nineteen

Maria and Sarah were walking down Nineteenth Street trying to catch a few tricks. But it was early, only 1:00 PM. The sun was shining; a brisk wind blew in from the North, slightly chilling one's ears, hands and ears.

They were headed to Andy's Corner Market to buy a couple of loosy's. Sarah scooped up her change and handed it to Maria. Maria counted it to a dollar fifty, enough for 3. If Maria were to flash him, they might get a 40-ounce to go with them.

Andy was Palestinian. Most of the corner stores were owned by Arabs as we called them.

The girls walked in. Maria was wearing a pair of Tommy jeans for girls. They pushed her normally flat ass up and in giving it a more full and rounded look. She pushed her already large full breasts up, arching her back, making them look even larger than what they were.

Sarah wore a pair of tight white pants that hugged her hips seductively and proudly displayed the thin bands of her white thong underwear.

"Hey Andy! How's it hanging?" asked Maria, the more forward of the two.

"It is hanging very nicely, fine thank you," Andy answered as he leaned over the counter so that he could get a better look at both girl's asses as they strolled by.

Sarah walked down one narrow aisle, and back another. Then stepped up to the counter.

"Andy, I need three loosy's please," she said as she spread the change on the counter.

Maria completed her scoping out of the store. It was empty except for them. She walked up to the counter next to Sarah and grabbed the bottom of her sweater. She raised it up, freeing her huge breasts. She plopped them on the counter.

Andy's eyes lit up, his mouth opened. He began rubbing his hands back and forth together as if they were suddenly cold.

"Andy, if I let you feel them, can we get two 40 ounces?"

Andy looked all around him, making sure that they were alone. Then he stuck both hands out reaching for her breasts.

Maria pulled back out of his reach, teasing him "Uhn, Uhn, Uhnnn! One 40, one tit. Two tits, two 40's, OK?"

She stood there massaging both breasts. She lifted one of her voluptuous breast up to her mouth and began licking her cherry sized nipple. Andy looked as if he was having a panic attack. He looked worse than a fiending crack head. He looked at Sarah and barely whispered, "Go, get the beer! Hurry!"

Maria stepped back up to the counter, sticking her breast back out for him to enjoy. Andy grabbed both breasts and began to gently squeeze them. His mouth opened. A string of saliva dripped from his mouth. He lowered his head and sucked one of her luscious nipples into his mouth. His left leg began to tremble.

"Heads up!" shouted Sarah.

Maria stepped back, pulling her blouse back into place. Andy stood upright and looked around to see who was coming. The door opened and four black girls came in.

"Hi Andy!" said a short light-skinned, well built girl. She wore a very expensive velour sweatsuit. Her hair was neat;

her nails were fresh with cubic zirconias implanted in every one.

Andy blushed as she came over and stood in front of him. Andy bagged up the two forty ounces and tossed in a pack of Newport 100's. He pushed the coins on the counter back to Sarah as if it was her change. Sarah picked up the package and quickly left the store. Maria closely followed. Sarah crossed the street with Maria still at her heels. They stepped into the Niagara Street Laundromat.

The laundromat was usually empty. It only had six of its eighteen washing machines in working order. Only three of the ten dryers worked too. Maria hopped on top of one of the out of order washers and grabbed a forty out of the bag. She cracked open the cap and turned the ice cold bottle up to her waiting lips. Sarah opened the pack of Newports and lit one up. She inhaled deeply then passed the cigarette to Maria.

"Maria, you think he's fucking that black chick?"

"Damn right he is! Did you see how that bitch was dressed? She's getting paid, swell!"

"Lucky ho," said Sarah as they continued to drink and smoke.

The door to the laundry opened. The four girls from Andy's stepped in. Sarah and Maria looked around. There was only one way out. The same door that the girls stood in front of. An uneasy feeling overcame them. Maria put their beer back into the plastic bag. Sarah lit up another cigarette, trying to hide her nervousness.

The short, cute, well dressed girl approached them. "Got another cigarette?" she asked.

Sarah held the pack out to her.

The girl took one and lit it. She inhaled deeply and blew the smoke into Sarah's face. She tilted her head back and sniffed. "Okay, which one of you funky white bitches is fuckin' my man?" she asked.

Maria and Sarah looked at each other and shrugged their shoulders. They simultaneously answered, "We don't know what you are talking about?"

"Don't fuckin' lie to me bitch! One of ya'll is fucking my man. Now which one of you is fucking him, dammit!"

As the cute girl stood there screaming on the two petrified white girls, the other three girls began removing earrings, necklaces and bracelets, preparing for battle.

Sarah saw that a fight was almost inevitable. "We have never fucked around with Andy. I swear it. We just tease him a little, that's all. But he never told us that he had a girl, just a frigid wife. He never ever mentioned you. If he had we wouldn't have ever teased him."

"Tease him! Tease him!! What the fuck did you do to tease him! I grabbed his dick and he had cum running all down his leg, and you want me to believe that all you did was tease him," screamed the cute black girl.

She charged at Sarah, grabbing her by her long blonde hair. Sarah tried to fight back but a bigger, stronger black girl came up and grabbed her arms preventing her from defending herself. Sarah was pulled to the ground. She looked for Maria, but she too was lying on the floor. Her arms were bent covering her face and head as the other two girls pounded on her.

They beat the two white girls down. Then they started ripping the girls' clothes off, wanting to see them naked.

Andy loved to put passion marks on the inside of girl's thighs. They were determined to see what marks, if any, could be seen. The white girls fought back as best they could, but soon they were naked.

"I don't see no marks, other than the ones that I put on this bitch," said Helen, the biggest and baddest of the bunch.

"This one is clean too!" said Rachel, the second largest.

"This is bullshit! I know that one of these bitches is fucking my man! I know it!" screamed Lakita, the cutest of the bunch.

Tonya, another extremely nice looking redbone went outside. She came back in carrying a broken broomstick. "I know how to find out what's going on. Let's beat it out of them." She handed the stick to Lakita.

Lakita walked over to the two naked white girls. They scurried together like they were trying to climb into each other's skin. Lakita raised the stick high in the air. A voice came from behind the girls.

"I hope that you're trying to scratch your back with that stick, Lakita!"

Lakita dropped the stick and turned around as if the devil herself had spoken to her.

"Sheka! What brings you in here. This ain't none of your business. These white hoes deserve this beat down."

Sheka stepped in followed by Pittsburgh, Detroit, New York, and little Amanda. Amanda came up and stood next to Sheka. Sheka looked over and asked Amanda, "Is that your Aunt Maria?'

Amanda shook her head yes, then ran over to her.

Maria and Sarah stood up trying to cover themselves with their hands. Sheka saw how hopeless it was for Maria to even partially cover those huge perfect tits.

"These girls need some clothes," said Sheka. She walked over to the frightened black girls. They'd all huddled together, standing behind Lakita.

Sheka's fighting prowess was well known. And by being backed by her crew, the black girls didn't want a confrontation. Fucking up two white hoes was one thing. Fighting Sheka's crazy ass was something else.

Sheka walked over to Lakita and ordered her and Rachel to strip and give their clothes to the naked white girls.

"Naw, Unh unhh! This sweatsuit cost $200. I ain't just gon' give it to this ho," shrieked Lakita.

"You're right bitch, 'cause you gonna give her those fancy sneakers too!" demanded Sheka.

"You gon' get yours one day Sheka. I swear you gon' get yours!" Lakita warned as she began to disrobe.

Detroit and New York stepped forward. "Is that a threat?" they asked.

No one answered.

Minutes later a bruised and battered Maria and Sarah walked out of the Laundromat, fully clothed and just as relieved.

Maria asked Amanda, "Who are you, and how do you know my name?"

Sheka burst out laughing. "You mean this ain't your Aunt Maria?"

Amanda joined in with the laughter.

A confused Sarah spoke up. "But how did you know that we were in here?"

"Let's just say that an Arabian bird told me," said Sheka as they walked past Andy's store.

Chapter Twenty

A tiny set of eyes peered through a thick pair of glasses across the street. Sheka and her crew of hoes were entertaining several young dope dealers from Buffalo. The tiny eyes closed. Jovanna thought to herself, *Damn, that light-skinned short nigga is so fine! Humpf! He could take my virginity anytime!*

Jovanna had just turned sixteen. But to see her, you'd think that she was at least twenty. She stood 5′8″ tall and weighed 140 pounds. Her breasts were full, rounded with nipples that were always hard. Her waist was small, flaring out into full, mature hips. Her face was narrow with high cheek bones and a keen nose. Her skin was a deep rich chocolate and her young face was blemish free. All of the men in the neighborhood were trying to get into her virgin panties.

With her eyes still closed, she slid her hand down her flat stomach into her pink ruffled panties. Her fingers sought that special place. Once it was found, she began to gently rub it in a circular motion. She reached behind her back and unsnapped her bra. The bra fell to the floor. She lifted her breast up to her shiny lips. Her tongue darted out, lapping at her black cherry sized nipple.

She imagined that the short light-skinned nigga from across the street was making love to her. Her fingers were working their magic. She was getting close. She fell back on the bed and opened her legs wider. She moaned. The door to her bedroom flew open!

"Jovanna! What the hell are you doing? It's the devil in you girl!! I will not have the devil in my house!!" barked Mrs. Carey

Mrs. Carey looked around the room for a weapon. She saw none. Mrs. Carey was a big woman. She stood two inches taller and a hundred pounds heavier than her daughter.

Deep wrinkles appeared in her otherwise smooth forehead. Sweat beads dropped down her temples. Her skin color darkened. A drop of saliva escaped her tight lipped mouth. She blocked the doorway. She stood there, staring with fist balled.

"Jovanna, I will not have the devil in my house." She stormed at the defenseless girl, pummeling her with a barrage of punches. Jovanna tried to cover up but her mother's huge fist pushed their way through.

"Get out devil!! Leave my house!! Leave it now!! I'm going to beat you back to hell!! You will leave my house!!!" She continued to beat her daughter senseless.

Jovanna screamed, "Stop momma, please stop. He's gone momma! The devil is gone!! You can stop momma! Please stop!!"

The young girl's pleas were stopped by a powerful fist to her mouth. Both lips burst, splattering blood everywhere.

Jovanna covered up as best she could and endured even more of the onslaught. For more than twenty minutes she beat her daughter with her fist. She beat her daughter like her father had beaten her. She stopped only from fatigue. Slowly, she pushed her largeness up off of the bed. She turned and slowly walked away, muttering to herself. "I won't have it! I just *won't* have it!"

The sound of the bedroom door shutting brought relief to Jovanna. She stayed lying on the bed curled in the fetal position, too sore to move. "That's it. That's the last time that she beats me. Tonight, I'm getting out of here." She stayed on the bed without moving an inch until she fell asleep, waiting on the night.

Sheka walked the five young men out to their money green Expedition. "You fellas be safe on y'all's trip back to Buff."

"Oh we will, Sheka. We gots to be safe, so we can come back to see you and yo hoes," said Sam, the youngest of the crew.

"Yo Sam, you ain't never had no pussy before yo young ass joined the crew, did you?" Marty was the oldest and biggest of the crew. He stood about 6'3" and weighed about 240 pounds. He was solid muscle. He'd done ten years at Leavenworth Federal Penitentiary where he developed his jailhouse physique.

The rest of the crew started ribbing on Sam. He climbed into the back of the cream colored interior of the truck and sank back into the plush leather seat. "Fuck y'all. I got game. I got mad game and mad hoes."

"Yeah, yo hoes is mad alright...mad 'cause they don't exist," Marty came back.

Sheka laughed and said, "Ya'll niggas is crazy. Leave Sam alone. He's cute."

After the last guy had climbed into the truck, they all kept fucking with Sam.

"Aw, he's cute."

"Sam is so damn cute."

"Sam! Why are you so damn cute?"

Sheka waved and backed away smiling, watching as the truck pulled away.

Jovanna hadn't left her room. She hadn't eaten nor bathed. Her backpack was stuffed with both pairs of her favorite shoes. She wore her sneakers, her jeans and top. Her pink sweatsuit and most of her underwear were placed in the backpack under her bed. She got into her bed, pulling the covers up tight around her neck. Tears began to run down the tracks on her face.

"No more. No more beatings mamma, no more."

At 2:00 AM, Mrs. Carey opened the bedroom door and peaked in on Jovanna. She appeared to be asleep. The door closed and Jovanna heard the familiar clink of the door being locked. Jovanna sprang out of bed. She ran over to the window and opened it. She threw her backpack out onto the roof of the porch and climbed out onto the roof.

She knew that she had to be careful. Her mother and father were in the room next door. She froze when the window was shut and the blinds to her mother's room were pulled closed. Several of the blinds were cocked allowing Jovanna a perfect view of what was going on inside. *Time to Window Shop.*

"That's it baby! Suck it. Suck it good Gloria."

Jovanna watched as her sanctified assed mother sucked her husband's dick with an expertise that one only acquires through years of experience.

"OK, Gloria, you know what I need." Mr. Carey pulled out of her mouth and lay back on the bed. He spread his legs, grabbing them at the knee and held them.

Gloria got on her knees and proceeded to lick her husband's hairy puckered ass as he began to masturbate.

Jovanna's mouth dropped. "Mom is a fucking hypocrite. Look at what she's doing. And she beat me for playing with myself. How disgusting!"

Jovanna watched as her father pulled her mother's head up. She opened her mouth just as he exploded in her face. She licked and sucked his dick until it was pristine clean shining with saliva.

She'd seen enough. She crawled over to the edge of the roof, and with her backpack in hand, she jumped.

Her landing was perfect. She threw the backpack over her shoulders and began to walk. She didn't know where she was going, nor did she care. All she knew was that she was never going back home. She turned down 24th Street heading toward the patch.

Chapter Twenty-One

Brigette was standing in front of the familiar lime green bungalow. She'd declined the offer of a ride in a limo. She wanted the time to think. She was nervous. More nervous than when she turned her first trick.

It had been five years. Tatiana was almost seven. *What could she say? What real reason can a mother have for abandoning her child?* Strawberry sucked it up and walked up to the door. Barking dogs could be heard coming from the backyard. She walked off the porch and went around back. Three huge black and red *Beware of Dog* signs lined the six foot red cedar fence. Brigette reached for the handle on the gate.

Both dogs began to growl and lunge at the back of the gate. Long, sharp fangs were bared as the hounds barked and growled ferociously at the small white hand that rested on the gate handle.

"Shh! Shhh, boys. It's only me. Remember me boys?" She pushed down on the handle, unlatching the gate.

"Shhh, General. Quiet Sarge. It's OK. I'm coming in." Brigette slowly pushed the gate open. The dogs barked even louder.

Just as Brigette was about to step through the opened gate, a child's voice rang out. "Sit down somewhere and be quiet!!" The child's voice was loud and shrill. But the dogs responded. Both dogs went to the child's side and obediently sat down.

"Excuse me, miss, but you shouldn't come back here without my mommy or my daddy being back here. My dogs bite people they don't know." The child grabbed the collars of both dogs as if she could possibly hold them if they had wanted to bolt.

"You must be Tatiana?" Brigette asked.

The curly haired, light-complexioned, gorgeous little girl blushed. "How did you know my name?"

"Oh, let's just say that we met a long time ago."

"When I was a little baby?"

"Something like that." Brigette slowly put her hand out in front of the shepherd huskie named General. He growled and stood at attention. His fangs bared. The hair around his neck was flared.

Tatiana tried to quiet him by tugging at his collar. Suddenly his ears dropped, and his tail began to wag. He began to wildly lick at Brigette's hand. She began rubbing behind his ears. General lunged at her, lapping wildly at her, pulling little Tatiana with him. They all fell to the ground. The larger of the two started jumping around and barking.

Nae Nae ran to the back door to see what the commotion was about. She stood there astounded at what she saw; Brigette, Tatiana and both dogs rolling around in the grass laughing their butts off. A wave of anger swept over her. "Tatiana!!! Get up from there!! Get up right this minute!!!"

Tatiana and Brigette both jumped up to their feet. Nae Nae stood in the doorway with both hands on her hips. "Tatiana, go in the house and get washed up for dinner."

"OK mommy," said Tatiana as she ran past Nae Nae and into the house.

Brigette stood there, not knowing what to do or say. General nudged her hand with his head still wanting to play.

"General! Go sit down somewhere!" shouted Nae Nae. General dropped his ears and curled his tail between his legs as he scurried away. Now both ladies were standing face to face. Both were silent.

A voice came from inside the door. "Nae Nae, what's going on out there? Tatiana said that we had company. Who's out there..."

The words hung on my tongue as I opened the screen door and saw Brigette standing there. She started brushing grass off of her stretch blue jeans. I watched as her hands started high on her flat tummy and down her firm thighs. Nae Nae followed my gaze.

"Well hello Brigette. Won't you please come in?" I held the door open as I invited Brigette in.

Nae Nae's stare could burn holes in stone. Her eyes followed Brigette's every move as she stepped inside. Brigette looked around. The house hadn't changed much at all.

"See Daddy, I told you that a pretty white lady was outside. She said that she met me when I was a little bitty baby?"

I looked at both of the women. "Yes baby, she met you when you were a little bitty baby," I answered.

"And then she left and is just now coming back. Things have sure changed since then. Tatiana is a big girl now. And Jessica was born and everybody is all very happy. Aren't we dear?" Nae Nae's comments hit home.

"It *was* nice to see you again Tatiana. But I'd best be going now," said Brigette as she started toward the door.

She was met by the prettiest little toddler that she'd ever seen. Almost copper in color with jet black curly hair and the whitest brightest eyes that she'd ever seen. She was standing directly in front of Brigette with her arms extended, asking to be picked up.

Without thinking twice about it, Brigette picked up the cute bundle of joy. Jessica laid her tiny head on Brigette's shoulder and grabbed a handful of Brigette's long golden braids.

"Look, Brigette, stay for dinner. Just like we'd planned. That way we can all get to know each other better," I said in an attempt to disarm the warming situation.

Tatiana ran over to Nae Nae and grabbed her hand. Yanking it softly, she asked, "Can the pretty lady eat with us mommy? Can she?"

Nae Nae looked over at Brigette, almost gloating. *She* was mommy, not Brigette. *She* was in control, not Brigette. *She* was Christopher's wife, *Not Brigette*. "Sure, Sure, she can stay for dinner." Nae Nae smiled as she headed into the dining room to set the table.

"Come on," said Tatiana as she grabbed Brigette's hand. "Come on so I can show you my room. I'm a big girl now. I sleep all by myself. Let me show you my room."

I watched as Brigette followed Tatiana up the stairs. Nae Nae watched me watch Brigette.

Chapter Twenty-Two

The police hadn't put much energy into solving Tiffany's death. Hell, she was just another white crackhead. Another statistic. As long as the number of crackheads stayed low, nobody gave a damn.

Black, T-Bone, Cleve, Steve and Stu were cruising the hood in their black Navigator. It was 9:00PM and just starting to get dark.

"Do y'all think this nigga is on the up and up?" asked Cleve. "A lot of times a nigga fresh out of the joint like that is dangerous."

"Dangerous. If that bitch ass nigga fucks with me, I'll show him who's dangerous," answered Black.

"But do you think that his story is on the up? He's supposed to know where a hundred keys are kept. What fool would let him know where that much dope is at?" Cleve pulled out a half smoked blunt and lit it. He took a deep drag off of it, waiting for a response.

"We about to find out. There go that nigga standing in front of Dunkin Donut, just like he said he would." Black swung the big black truck up into the parking lot.

Babybra, a 5'8", 190 pound, dark-skinned, bald headed, muscular young man was standing in front of the side doorway to the restaurant. A huge white smile came across his face as soon as he saw the large 4x4. Babybra ran over to the parked truck and hopped in.

"Goddamn! Every time I get in this bitch, I get excited. Are you really going to give this to me and you gonna pay it off like you said?"

Black turned around and faced the young man. "I'll give you this truck *and* $50,000 cash money if what you say pans out."

"Oh, it's there. I know it's there. And I know who it belongs to too."

"Well after tonight, it belongs to us," snickered Steve.

"How'd you find out about this stash?" Asked Black.

"Remember a skinny ho named Nina? Well one night Nina was coming from the patch over to my house to trick. I'd just come home good and I needed to get off real bad.

"Anyway, she walked past the carwash on 11th Street, and she saw two Jamaicans and two niggas taking the shit off of a boat and loading it into a Suburban. She ran to my house and made me go back with her so that I could believe what she'd seen. But by the time that I got there, they were just finishing up. I recognized both Jamaicans and one of the other niggas. The light-skinned dude was Geno, Geno Johnson."

"I know that nigga Geno. He's a partner in that limousine service on Main Street," shouted T-Bone.

"I think we all know Geno, but where's the shit?"

"It's on Tennessee Avenue, at the Jamaicans' house. They keep it there 'til Geno wants it."

"Do you know which house on Tennessee?"

"I sure do. Seems like those Jamaicans like pussy too. Nina has tricked there with both of them. 903 Tennessee. That's where they live, 903."

Black pulled off headed for Tennessee. When he got to Virginia Avenue, he pulled over and parked. "You niggas ready," he asked as he pulled out and inspected two loaded nine millimeters.

Several guns could be heard clicking as they were all checked for readiness

"Ready boss," joked Steve.

"So let's do it." Black pulled off and rounded the corner of Tennessee Avenue. He parked two houses down from 903.

"Come on baby brother, I need you to go ask for Nina."

"But I thought that all I had to do was show you. I don't want no part of taking it." Babybra's voice quivered as he spoke.

"Too late," said Cleve as he pushed the bigger, Babyboy out of the truck. "And remember, I got my shit aimed at you!"

Reluctantly, Babybra led Cleve toward the alley. They hit the alley and walked up to the side door of the spot. Black rang the doorbell. Nobody answered. He rang the bell again. *Ding dong, ding dong.* He pressed his ear to the door. The sound of scurrying feet could be heard inside.

He rang the bell again.

Suddenly the door flew open. A bearded dread wearing a Jamaican headwrap stood in the doorway. "What ygwon! What be you ringing me bell like dat?"

Babybrother stepped up. "H-Have you seen Nina? I need to see Nina if she's here. Please."

"No Nina's here. So be gone mon."

Black stepped in and pressed the barrel of his nine millimeter in the Jamaican's face.

"You know what time it is."

"Do you know what you be doing?"

"We'll soon find out, won't we?" Black pushed the Jamaican back into the house. Babybrother motioned for the other men that were waiting in the truck.

T-Bone, Cleve, Steve and Stu ran and burst through the side door with guns drawn. They stormed in the living room where the second Jamaican sat on the sofa smoking a fat blunt.

Black pushed the first Jamaican on the couch with the second one. The second one kept right on smoking his blunt, smiling.

"What the fuck is so damn funny, fool? Don't you know that you're about to die?" asked Cleve as he aimed his tech-9 at dude.

Black walked over and shot the first Jamaican in the leg. He recoiled in pain, clutching his bleeding leg.

"Fucking blood clot!! Me hopes you rot in hell!!" shouted the bleeding man.

"You first," said a laughing Steve as he blew the man's head off with a blast from his 12-gauge. Blood and brain matter blew all over the sofa and floor.

Before Steve could react, the man was off of the sofa and had landed a solid kick to Steve's head knocking him clear out of the room. Spinning around on one arm like a wild break dancer, Dreadman kicked Steve in the groin, then Babybrother in the knee, breaking it. Yard man landed on his feet ready to attack, when Stu cracked his head open with the butt of his M-16.

"Find the shit and let's get the fuck out of here," said Black.

T-Bone and Stu ran to the basement and opened it.

Pow, Pow, Pow! Pop, Pop, Pop. Pop, Pop Pop! Shots came from the basement. Black and the rest of the crew ran to the top of the stairs. Three dead pit bulls lay on the floor.

T-Bone and Stu began dragging the two large dark green footlockers toward the stairs. Black and Steve each grabbed a handle and they carried the footlockers outside.

Cleve was helping Babybrother out to the truck. "Wait a minute fellows, I got something to do." Cleve grabbed a glass of watered down iced tea from off of the coffee table and tossed it in the Jamaican's face. The man came to, swinging and kicking.

Cleve pulled out a glock and put ten quick ones into the Jamaican's body. "I guess you won't kick me no more now, will you?"

"Come on niggas, let's get the fuck up out of here," screamed Steve as he helped Cleve carry Babybrother out to the truck.

Soon they were loaded up and heading home.

"That bitch busted my knee. He busted my fucking knee. How I'm gon' drive. How is I'm gon' drive?

"Yeah man, he fucked you up pretty good. What was that shit he was doing? What do you call that shit?" asked Steve.

"I don't know, but he was a bad mothafucka with it," laughed Stu.

"No, he's a *dead* mothafucka with it! He kicked me in my prized jewels, the bitch," said Cleve as he gently held his sore balls.

They pulled up into Black's driveway and struggled to get the trunks into the house. After taking Babybrother to the hospital, they left Stu at the hospital with Babybrother and went back to examine the goods.

Steve pulled up one of the trunks and opened it. "Goddamn!! Mothafucka!!" Steve screamed and reached for his gun.

Sitting in the trunk on top of stacks of coke, was a 16-foot boa constrictor.

Black grabbed a meat cleaver from off of the kitchen counter and hacked the snake into several pieces. "No guns! No guns in my house ever!" he shouted. "Let's clean this shit up and see what we've got."

They counted up 25 kilos in the trunk. Nobody wanted to open the next trunk. Black finally kicked it open. They found another snake only a little larger. Black chopped him up too. There was 25 kilos in that trunk as well.

"I thought that he said that there were 100 keys," asked Black.

"That's all that was down there Black. Just these two trunks," claimed T-Bone. T-Bone sat down on Black's sofa, smiling, wondering how Stu was going to react when he got the *other* two trunks and opened them. Stu was deadly afraid of snakes.

Chapter Twenty-Three

Geno was furious. Rice was standing in front of him after explaining that the dope was gone and that both Jamaicans were dead.

"I want my shit! I don't give a fuck about your dead Jamaican bitches. I just want my shit!!" Geno was screaming at the top of his lungs. "I spent $10,000 per key, 100 keys. That's a fucking million dollars. Did you hear me? A fucking millions dollars!!!"

"Geno, I'll find out what happened. You know how the ghetto is. Niggas can't do shit like this without somebody talking about it."

"You'd better find out, and find out fast. I want my shit!"

"Give me a couple a' days. That's all I need is a couple a' days."

"I'll do better than that. You've got 'til Monday. But Monday morning, I want my shit." Geno walked over and rubbed his bald head while looking in the mirror that overlooked the mantle of the fireplace. He adjusted his glasses and left without saying another word.

Rice went into the bedroom. "Yo shorty! Wake up!"

Jovanna stirred and pulled the cover up tightly around her neck. She yawned. Without thinking another thought, she sat up exposing her nakedness. Large firm breasts, a small tight waist that led to wide full hips. Her rich chocolate skin glistened under the sunlight that flickered through the window that Rice had opened.

Rice walked over and tossed ten twenty dollar bills on the bed. "It's time to bounce, shorty. It was fun, but like they say, all good things come to an end.'

"Do I have to go? I'll stay for free. I don't have any place else to go."

"Not my problem, sweetheart. I ain't captain save-a-ho or nothing. It's time to bounce!"

Rice's cell phone rang.

"Hello."

"What's up dawg?" answered Cedric.

"What's up ma nigga?"

"We ain't heard from you in a couple a' days. Jus' checkin' to make sure you alright, that's all."

"Yeah, um cool. Ben chillin' with a fresh honey, that's all." Rice looked over at Jovanna as she started to get dressed. She struggled to get her tight jeans up over her firm, wide ass. *Damn! she was built.* Not knowing that he was watching, she wiped a tear from her face while continuing to get dressed

"Yo Ced, let me get back with you. Hey, thanks for checking up on a nigga. I'll be at the spot some time today and smoke one wit' a nigga." Rice closed his cell phone before Cedric could finish his sentence.

"Yo shorty, what's up with the tear game?" Rice said as he walked over and spun Jovanna around facing him. "Huh? What's up with the tear game shorty?"

"It ain't no game, and my name ain't shorty," she cried as she spoke. The eye damns burst. Tears covered her face.

"Shorty look, a nigga can't let a ho stay around too long. Soon as a nigga start feelin' a ho, she always bounce on him. That's why a nigga got to kick a ho to the curb first."

"Oh! So you was startin' to feel me?"

Rice paused. "Yeah. Yeah, I was starting to feel you. Damn girl! You young, you fine as hell and last night when you cooked dinner and cleaned the crib, a nigga started thinking about how nice it would be to have a shorty around. You know, for real.

"Then it kicked in on how I picked you up on 10th Street, the patch you know. A nigga can't get crazy."

"Oh, being with me is crazy? It's OK to fuck the shit out of me but not care? Fuck me, I'm just a ho! Right? Right?"

Her tears continued to pour.

Rice lifted her chin with the crook of his index finger. He wiped the tears away. Their eyes locked. "Look shorty, you can stay 'til Monday. Then we'll get you some place safe."

Jovanna threw her arms around him, pressing her breast deep into his chest. She thought to herself, *You were the first, the only man that I've ever had. I'm not a ho.*

Rice lifted her up by the cheeks of her ass and kissed her full on the mouth. She wrapped her legs around him. *What's wrong with me,* he thought, *I never kiss a ho! What's wrong with me?* Moments later he was deep inside her, pumping as if his life depended on it.

Stokes came out of the side door of the four suite apartment building carrying a brown paper bag. He walked across the busy street and over to a parked red escort with Canadian plates on it. The rear door opened and he stepped in.

"Did you get it?"

"Stokes always gets what Stokes promises."

"Let me see it?" asked Patsy as she nervously reached for the brown paper bag that Stokes was still clutching tightly.

She opened the bag and took out a pearl handled chrome plated .32 caliber automatic pistol. Her fingers danced over the shiny chrome. The gun fit perfectly inside her hand.

Teri and Tara both leaned in, closely examining the gun as if were a gift for Christmas.

"Ooh! It's pretty. It's real pretty!" exclaimed Tara.

"It's pretty alright! And deadly too," said Stokes as he took a box of .32 caliber hollow point bullets out of the bag and handed them to Patsy.

"How do I load it?" she asked.

Stokes removed the clip and loaded the clip. He slowly fed the clip back into the gun and flicked the safety on.

"Here, it's ready to fire, but let Stokes out before you take that safety off. Stokes don't want to be no accident."

All of the girls started laughing. Patsy placed the loaded gun into her purse and handed Stokes a crisp big face fifty dollar bill.

"You sure you wouldn't rather have one of us?" she asked, trying to sound sexy.

"No thank you, Stokes is gonna keep this money for awhile, so's Stokes can figure out what he want to spend it on."

They watched as Stokes folded the bill very meticulously and placed it inside of an old brown leather tobacco pouch. He then tucked the pouch into his soiled jacket pocket.

"Stokes thanks you pretty ladies, but it's time for Stokes to go. There's a lot of money lying around in bottles and cans for Stokes to get." Stokes smiled, opened the door to the car and got out.

Once he was gone, Teri yapped, "Why didn't you just break him off a piece of rock?"

"Because he did us a favor. You don't go around fucking over everybody that you meet. The deal was for fifty dollars, so that's what he gets," barked Patsy.

"Why *not* fuck over somebody else, everybody tries to fuck over us."

"Teri, I'm done with it. Tara, let's go."

Tara started up the car. "Where to, Patsy?" she asked.

"Let's just cruise the patch. Maybe we'll be lucky enough to run across those bastards that got us."

Tara pulled off and headed toward the patch.

Chapter Twenty-Four

Brigette had only stayed the one night at the Daniel's residence. The awkwardness of being there with Nae Nae had outweighed the joy of seeing Tatiana.

They'd decided not to tell Tatiana that Brigette was her birth mother. Not yet anyhow. Since Brigette had hit the Falls, she'd only gone to two NA meetings. She felt herself beginning to fall off.

She couldn't sleep at all. She had tossed and turned for hours. She wondered what time it was. She looked at the clock on the nightstand, 3:01 AM. Before she could stop herself she was dressed and out of her room. The receptionist was fast sleep. Brigette slipped past her and out the front door. She ran up to Tenth Street and quickly turned and headed for the Patch. She kept a brisk pace as she made her way.

"Yo, little mama, need a ride back to Buffalo?"

Moonlight gleamed across his pearly white teeth as he spoke. His voice was pleasant, almost friendly. She was sure that she'd heard it before she was standing on the edge of the patch. She inhaled deeply. Damn, she wanted to get high. She needed the rush, the temporary escape.

"Yo, snowflake! What's up? Remember us? The taxi ride from Buff?" This voice was also familiar. Of course! The two men from McDonalds in Buffalo. She stopped, making sure that it was just the two of them.

The passenger door opened and the tall one named Anthony stepped out. "Would you like a ride miss?" This was perfect. They were safe and they were loaded. She could smell the mixture of weed and liquor even from where she stood.

She answered without even thinking, "Sure, why not."

She slid into the seat next to Kenny. His eyes widened as her short, white skirt rode up her milky thighs. She made no effort to pull it down.

"Where to?" asked Anthony as he stepped back into the car and closed the door. Brigette lay her hand high up on his thigh saying, "Anywhere that your money can take you?" She leaned over and nibbled playfully on his ear.

"Kenny, let's go to my crib," suggested Anthony.

"Naw, mine is closer."

"Fellas! Fellas! Let's go to your crib tonight Anthony. And your crib tomorrow!" She leaned over and blew softly into Kenny's ear.

"Goddamn!" screamed Anthony as he accelerated the car, hurrying to get to Kenny's crib.

Within minutes they were stepping into Kenny's superbly furnished house.

"Wow! This place is enormous! And you live here alone?" asked Brigette as she walked around admiring the mahogany Old English style tables and the bone colored handmade sofas and chairs. She ran her fingers across the keys of the walnut upright piano.

Kenny was stripping as he headed up the walnut staircase. The front of his pants was sticking out eight inches ahead of him.

"Come one, let's have some fun," said Anthony as he held his hand out for hers. She placed her tiny hand in his and followed him up the stairs.

The door to one of the four bedrooms was wide open. They laughed as they watched Kenny's wide ass disappear under the green satin sheets.

They walked in still holding hands.

"Can I have a drink, some weed, anything to loosen me up a little?" she asked.

"Sure baby, we've got it all! You name it. We've got it!" shouted Kenny from the bed. He leaned over, opened a drawer on the nightstand next to the bed and pulled out a plate filled with goodies.

Weed, E, Crystal Meth, Viagra, a straight shooter and an eight ball of crack. A rush came over her. Her mouth became dry. Her stomach tightened and the palms of her hands became wet.

Anthony handed her a lighter. She picked up the pipe and the eight ball. "Where's the restroom at?"

Anthony walked over to what she thought was a closet door and opened it. A huge pink and black bathroom was behind it. Brigette went into the restroom and closed the door.

Anthony put on an old Bob James classic, the theme from Taxi. He picked up his cell phone and pushed the number 3 speed dial on his cell phone. The voice on the other end was weak and shaky as if she was whispering.

"Hello?"

"She's here!"

"What?"

"She's here. Get here now!"

"Wha- Where? Oh! OK!" *Click.*

Anthony closed his cell phone and began to undress.

Twenty minutes later, Brigette stepped out, naked. She walked over and climbed into the bed between the two erect men. She grabbed a penis in each hand and began to slowly masturbate them. Anthony gently removed her hand and led her by the back of her head down to his rock hard dick. She rose to her knees, aiming her luscious ass in Kenny's face. Kenny got on his knees behind her and entered her tight pussy from behind. He began a slow grind against her round firm bottom. She went to work on Anthony's dick, showing him her best techniques. His balls began to swell, and he knew that he wouldn't last long, so he pulled away.

Kenny was beginning to tire. He pulled out and lay flat on the bed. He motioned for Brigette to mount him, which she did. She began to bounce up and down on him with all that she had. Anthony stood in the middle of the bed and stuck his dick in her mouth. She sucked him off in seconds. His come shot all over her face and hair. Then Kenny came, shooting deep inside of her womb.

Anthony saw a bright light flickering underneath the door. Suddenly, the door flew open and the bright light hit them. Everyone froze.

Then Brigette realized that they were being filmed. She tried to cover her face. Her hands became covered with wet sticky cum. She tried to jump up out of the bed, but both men held her tight.

They began to smile and pose for the camera. The filming had stopped. "Thank you, gentlemen. Thank you very much!! You have no idea what this means to me," said Nae Nae as she tossed a stack of hundreds on the bed. "Please pay her well. It looks like she was worth it. Good morning Brigette. I don't think that I have to say what will happen with this film if you ever stick your whorish white ass around my husband or my house again. Do I make myself clear? Thank you and goodnight."

Nae Nae walked out of the room smiling.

"Anything for a sister, sister."

"Sister? What do you mean sister?" asked Brigette in between a barrage of tears.

"That's my sister. My blood sister. We have different fathers but we have the same mother. Plus, she's black, little mama. And we always goes with our own. Always!" said Anthony.

Brigette flopped back down on the bed. *Now what,* she thought *Now what?*

Kenny was hard again and motioned for her to give him some head. She reached over and took three hundred-dollar bills off of the stack and put them in the pocket of her white skirt. Then she took Kenny's hard dick into her mouth and began giving him pleasure.

Chapter Twenty-Five

Stu had damn near shit his pants when he opened the two trunks and found the ten-foot boa constrictors inside. He beat them to death with a baseball bat, splattering cocaine powder all over the place.

When T-Bone caught up with him he cursed him out.

"You dumb mothafucka. I could have been killed. Why didn't you tell me that those fuckin' snakes were in there?"

"I didn't know big boy. Now calm down, calm down baby. And think about all the money that we are about to make. We're going to be rich!"

"OK, we got the shit. Now how are we gon' dump this shit?"

"No problem. No problem at all. Do you remember Moe and Solo, two of Geno's old crew? Well, they felt as if Geno set them up. So they sent us some old school style niggas. Some niggas that'll blow this city up.

"One of them they call Stunner. The other they call D-Nice. Moe said that we can put it all in to their hands and sit back."

"What! Give them all of this shit and sit back. Is Moe crazy?"

"Yeah and so is Solo, but I'm true to the game not new to the game, so I'm following their suggestion."

"Why can't we sell it?"

"Because, we can't explain where we got it without drawing suspicion to the big robbery. And in case you've forgotten, two men are dead."

Stu stood up and began to pace around in the room of the Niagara Hotel. Both trunks full of cocaine sat in front of them.

T-Bone's cell phone rang.

"Hello."

"Is this T-Bone?"

"Who wants to know?"

"This is D-Nice from Atlantic City. Some very good men sent me down. I'm looking for employment. Can you suggest anyone for me?"

"I can do better than that. Meet me at the corner of 58th and Buffalo Avenue."

"I'm on my way." Click

T-Bone looked over at Stu and said, "It's Showtime!"

Stu was busy re-stacking the bricks of cocaine. Several bricks had burst when he killed the snakes. He took huge chunks and stuffed his pockets with them as he rewrapped the damaged packages.

Minutes later...

Stu led both men into their hotel suite. The trunks sat stacked by the doorway. D-Nice was a short powerfully built man. He was medium complexioned, bald and had eyes that never stopped probing.

He spoke with a busted jersey accent and finished every sentence with the phrase, "Knowa'I mean?"

The Stunner man was built like a wrestler. Short, stocky, light-skinned and had waves so deep that they made you sea sick. He closely resembled his dead cousin.

Each man grabbed a trunk and headed out of the door.

"Thank you gentlemen. We'll be getting in touch as soon as we've done something substantial, knowa'I mean?"

Stu stood there, not wanting his dope out of his sight. He didn't really trust anybody, let alone somebody that he didn't know. He patted his packed pockets and smiled. At least he got enough to put a little change in his pocket.

T-Bone had walked out to the Astro Minivan that the men drove. Once the trunks were loaded into the van and the men were gone, he walked back into the motel room.

"Good news, Stu. They practically guaranteed us a mil. Do you hear that? Five hundred thousand each. You are about to be a very wealthy man."

"Yeah, I'll believe it when the money is in my hands."

"Look nigga, for the last time. Moe and Solo said that these nigga are thoroughbreds. So let's wait and let them work."

Stu continued to protest for awhile before finally storming out of the door.

T-Bone stripped and showered. After he showered and changed clothes, he went about gathering his belongings from the floor. While picking up the last item, a sock, he noticed a powdery substance splatter on the rug.

"What the fuck!" He picked up a small chunk and rubbed it on his gums. "Coke!" he cried and then wondered what Stu was up to...

• • •

Geno was sitting inside of the stretch Hummer watching a bootleg stag DVD that someone had left in the Hummer after a night on the town.

"Geno!"

"I'm in here Mr. Daniels," he answered.

The DVD started to play. A black guy was fucking the shit out of a white girl from behind.

"Mr. Daniels, come look at this. Ain't this that nigga Cleve from over on the South side?"

I climbed into the back of the Hummer and sat down on the plush leather seat next to Geno. "Is what who?" I asked.

"Cleve, ain't that Cleve from over on Willow Avenue?"

I sat back just in time to see another nigga lead a big pit bull up and onto the white girls upturned ass. The dog began to fuck the upturned ass as fast as he could.

"Damn, ain't that Black's dog, Bruno? Hell yeah, that's him. That dog don' won me thousands. I'd know that dog anywhere!" screamed Geno

We both watched as the canine carried on with his assault. The camera slowly turned until the girl's face came into view. A sock hung from her mouth. Her eyes were bucked open. Terror was wielded on her face.

"Tiffany! Pause the video! That's Tiffany! I'm positive of it."

"Tiffany? Who the fuck is Tiffany?" asked Geno.

"You remember Tiffany, Brigette's friend. The one that turned her out. The one that they found dead a couple of weeks ago."

"Naw, that ain't her. She's too skinny."

"Look nigga, I've fucked that bitch enough times to know her naked ass when I see her."

The film continued. The girl continued to move. We couldn't tell if she was struggling or enjoying it. Then she got wilder and wilder then...nothing. She topped moving altogether. The video ended.

"Was she dead?" I asked.

"I don't know. I don't even know if that was her or not, Mr. Daniels."

"Brigette'll know. If anybody would know, *she* would."

"We'll call her and I'll go pick her up Mr. Daniels. Let's find out. Let's find out right now."

I whipped out my cell phone and called the Mission. Brigette had moved out days before. She left no forwarding address. Disappointed, I hung up.

"I don't know where she is. She left the mission."

"Well let me see if I can find her, Mr. Daniels. I'll call you if I do."

"OK Geno. Call me. I've gotta stop in at home for a minute. I'll be back to close up."

I climbed out of the Hummer and jumped into a black Lincoln Towncar and pulled out heading home.

Chapter Twenty-Six

Nae Nae had taken the kids over to the babysitter's house. She'd showered and put on a long white sheer negligee, complete with a pair of crotchless panties. Several scented candles were lit throughout the house. A fire log was just beginning to burn inside of the fireplace. All of the drapes and blinds were drawn.

A bottle of Welch's grape juice and a bottle of Dom Perignon were being chilled in the double ice bucket. A prescription bottle of Viagra lay next to it. She dabbed a little of my favorite oil, *Eat it Raw* on the insides of her thighs. Nae Nae started to pace nervously around in the living room.

A bag of weed and strawberry wrap appeared out of her purse. Nifty fingers rolled it. Experienced lungs inhaled and held the strong acrid smoke. Slowly, she exhaled and enjoyed the light headed feeling that overcame her. She stared at her watch. *He should have been here twenty minutes ago.*

She picked up the house phone, then sat it back down. She started talking to herself. "Now be smart about this girl. He's *your* husband. He sleeps with *you* in *your* bed, *every* night. Well almost every night he's not working. And she's a *white* ho! I ain't got nothing to worry about. Not from her anyway!"

I drove all over town looking for Brigette. I sat in front of known crack houses and circled the patch for over an hour.

I asked every ho that I saw about her whereabouts. But no one had seen her.

I looked at my watch. 5:00 PM. *Damnit! I'm late.* I called Geno and asked him if he would close up shop for me. Then I sped home. The house was closed up tight. If I hadn't seen Nae's car, I might've kept on going.

After parking I went through the side door. The faint aroma of weed and apple cinnamon from the burning candles crept up into my nostrils. The sounds of Luther Vandross tricked down from upstairs. I followed the sounds. They came from my bedroom. I eased open the door and stepped in.

Lying in the middle of our bed was Nae Nae. Her skin tight negligee hugging her like a gloved hand holding her in place. She was fast asleep. The bottle of Dom was half empty. Two blunt roaches set in the ashtray on the nightstand. I felt sorta bad for being late. The bottle of Viagra set on the nightstand too. I grabbed the bottle of 100 milligram pills and popped one. Then I opened the bottle of chilled grape juice and poured myself a glass.

I undressed and stepped into the shower. When I was fresh and clean I dried myself off and went back into the bedroom naked. Crawling on to the bed I lifted the hem of the negligee and eased my head in between Nae Nae's legs. I kissed each thigh. Nae Nae began to squirm, opening her legs more. Now there was enough room for my entire head to ease up under her shear clothed body. I ran my tongue up to the opening of her crotchless panties.

Nae Nae opened her legs wide and began to grind into my face as my tongue found its mark. The scent of my woman aroused me. I felt myself growing harder and longer. The 100's had kicked in. I was more than ready.

Nae Nae awakened with a smile on her face. Her man was home. She would now do all of the things for me that I liked. She would please me orally first, vaginally next and lastly, she would let me have her tight asshole. I loved coming up her sweet tight ass.

Yes, tonight was going to be our night. She'd call later and tell Lisa that she'd pick the kids up in the morning.

• • •

Geno closed up the shop and jumped into his 2005 platinum Lexus. He rode up and down every street in the hood looking for Brigette. While riding up Highland Avenue, Geno noticed several people talking to a new guy in the area. Several of these guys were small time dealers. Men that bought anywhere from a half ounce to a quarter key. He watched as a light-skinned stocky man with deep set waves served each and every man. Another man, a brown-skinned short, thickly muscled dude seemed to be the lookout.

Who are these guys? And where did they get their dope? Was it my missing shit?

Geno decided to go check the new niggas out. He pulled down the street and parked right across from the dealers. "The best way to find out is to see for yourself."

So he walked up to the light-skinned fellow. "What's up?" asked Geno.

"The sky, if you're looking."

"What I mean is, who are you guys with?"

"What is it to you?"

"Well, I know everybody in this city, but I don't know you!"

"Now why would you want to know me?'

"I need to know who I'm buying a kilo of powder from."

"You got $22,500 cash?"

"You got a kilo of powder?"

"I thought that *I* asked the questions?"

"Not with my money you don't."

"Let's go inside and talk to my partner."

"Hold on. Let me get the money." Geno went to the trunk of his car and opened a brown leather attaché case. Inside was $25,000 cash and a loaded 9mm.

He closed the case and lifted it out of the trunk. The light-skinned man led him inside of a dumpy looking two-family house. D-Nice sat in what should have been the living room. But instead of furniture, the entire room was filled with pillows. Pillows of every size, shape and color. Several pillows were stacked to form a throne. D-Nice sat in the middle of them.

"Well, hello Geno! I was wondering when we would meet. This is even sooner than I'd expected."

"How do you know who I am?"

"I make it my business to research before I get into anything, knowa-I-mean? That's how I operate."

"Well now that you know me, who are you?"

"My name is D-Nice and this is the real number one Stunner not like that made for TV nigga. He's for real though, knowa-I-mean?"

No, Geno didn't get what he meant, but he was about to find out. Geno set his attaché case on one of the huge pillows in the middle of the floor. He unlocked both sides of it simultaneously.

The one called the *Stunnerman* swiftly leaped in the air landing on top of the brown leather case. Before Geno could move the stocky man was upon him. D-Nice got up from his throne of pillows and walked over to them. He removed the attaché case from under stunner's foot and opened it.

He pulled the pistol out and waved it at Geno. "I assume that this is for your protection, know-I-mean? You hadn't planned on using it to attack me with, had you? 'Cause that would be a very bad thing, know I mean?"

Geno didn't know how to respond, so he remained silent.

The stunner man counted the stacks of cash. $22,500.

"It's exactly enough for a brick, Dee. Think he was on the level, or do you think he was going to try us?"

"Well if you ask me? Knowa-I-mean? I think that this wimp was going to try us. And that pisses me off. Knowa-I-mean? It pisses me off real bad!"

Thirty minutes later...

D-Nice and Stunner dragged a heavy trunk out to the van and loaded it into it. The next morning several reports were made of a large green trunk going over the Falls.

Chapter Twenty-Seven

Night time on the patch was the highlight of a lot of people's lives. Most of the strawberries made a majority of their money once the sun had fallen. Short skirts, tight pants and daisy dukes that looked as if they were painted on filled the dark cool nights. Nickel and dime drug dealers stood in groups on the corners talking shit and sharing blunts and 40-ounce bottles of beer. One out of every four cars either stopped for dope or to haggle price with one of the dozens of hoes. Beats flooded the air as Niggas bounced their heads and clapped their hands to the likes of *50 Cent, The Game,* and *Kanye West.*

Almost every night was like a huge street party. The police would cruise through every hour on the hour, ignoring what they could. Hell, they didn't care. It was mainly niggas killing niggas. They killed with drugs, guns and AIDS. Their thinking was that if they kept most of the niggas huddled together like that, they would eventually kill themselves off.

Babybrother came cruising through the patch in his newly acquired black Navigator. He had 2G's in his pockets. A far cry from the $25,000 that he was promised, but he was satisfied. His system was bumping as he slowed down to a crawl so that he could check out the hoes.

Cedric, Cobbs, and Rice were sitting in their red Escalade smoking a blunt as BabyBoy cruised by. "Hey, ain't that that nigga that just got out of jail? What's his name? Um, Big Baby...No, Baby Boy. That's it. His name is BabyBoy, Ain't that him in Black's truck?" asked Cobbs.

"Yeah, that's him. But I heard that Black sold it to him. At least that's the word on the street," added Rice

"Is Black doin' that bad?"

"Better question is, where did Babyboy get the money to buy it?" Cedric turned his radio down as if the quiet would allow him to think better.

"Come on, Scott, pass the mothafuckin' blunt." Rice leaned back over the headrest reaching for the blunt. Scott playfully passed the burning blunt to Cedric who was sitting in the driver's seat. Cedric took the blunt and inhaled deeply. He blew the smoke in Rice's direction.

"See, you niggas play too much! When y'all gon' grow up? Y'all act like a bunch of kids."

"Yeah nigga, like the one that you've been keeping at your crib?" answered Cobbs.

"Uh huh, we know all about your sixteen year-old ho."

"Sixteen! Who said that she was sixteen," cried Rice.

"Come on, man. Where've you been? Everybody knows that that sixteen year-old runaway is at your crib."

"Runaway! I didn't know that she was no runaway. I picked her up on the stroll. She was working the patch! I swear it!"

"She might'a been walking *through* the patch because she didn't have no place to go late at night."

"But she fucked the shit out of me, and she sucks dick like a pro."

"Yeah, yeah. My cousin Tashawn says that every nigga in high school been tryin' to hit it. Nobody ever has."

"You mean she was a virgin?"

"Word!"

"Naw, you niggas fuckin' with my head that's all. Ya'll just fuckin' with a nigga!" Rice didn't want to say it, but it made sense. She was much *too* fine to be out on the stroll without a habit. Only crack could drive someone like her to the drudgery of the patch.

"Ced, drop me at the crib. I can't have no underage runaway holding up at my crib."

"Nigga that young bitch got 'chu pussy whipped!" laughed Cobbs.

"Nigga please! I don't fall for no ho! I find 'em, fuck 'em and forget 'em! I'm a player. I don't get played!" answered Rice trying to be cool.

Ced started up the truck and pulled off down Tenth Street heading toward Rice's crib. Rice jumped out as soon as they pulled in front of his apartment. He stormed toward his door and burst through it like a man on fire.

The smell of fresh cooked collard greens, corn bread and fried chicken attacked his nostrils. The apartment was meticulously cleaned. He walked through the living room and into the kitchen. The faint smell of Pine Sol lingered in the air. He stopped and called out to her. "Hey shorty, get out here."

He looked on top of the stove. Several pots were sitting in the flickering eyes, keeping the food warm. He checked each pot. Corn on the cob, collard greens cooked with smoked turkey neck bones, baby limas cooked in salt, pork, fried chicken and his favorite Jiffy cornbread.

Jovanna came running into the kitchen wearing only panties and a bra. "Yes baby? Did you call?"

"Yeah I called. Go put some clothes on. We gotta talk!"

"Talk about what baby? Did I burn something? Did I do something wrong?"

Rice took a deep breath. He stared at the floor. This was going to be harder than he thought. *Damnit! Why did she have to try so fucking hard! Why did she have to be so fuckin' fine?*

Jovanna went back into the bedroom and put on a pair of tight fitting jeans and a top.

"Sit down," he ordered.

They both sat down at the kitchen table.

Jovanna looked around and realized that the burners were still on. She got up and turned them off.

"How old are you? And are you a runaway?'

She didn't answer.

"I asked you a question. I need to know these things. What if 5-0 was to roll up on me? I could go to jail for harboring a runaway, statutory rape, contributing to the delinquency of a minor and who knows what else. Plus, we've been fucking raw dog. What if you were to get pregnant?"

She still made no comment.

"Shorty, you've got to go! I'm sorry, but you've got to go."

Tears started to fall from her face. But she made no sound. Slowly she got up and took a plate from the cabinet. She filled the plate with something out of each pot. Taking a tall glass from another shelf, she filled it with ice and iced tea which she set in front of Rice, and then she disappeared into the bedroom.

Before he could finish his meal, the bedroom door opened and Jovanna stepped out. She'd cut a pair of her jeans into ultra short daisy dukes. The bottoms of the cheeks of her firm ass hung below the hem of the shorts. Her blouse was tied at the waist, showing off her flat belly and ample breasts.

As she headed toward the door carrying everything that she owned in a backpack, she stopped leaned over and kissed Rice on the top of his head. "Goodbye, baby," was all that she said.

"Jovanna, was I really the first?"

She opened the door and stepped out. Before she shut the door, she answered him. "What do you think, baby? What do you think?"

And she was gone.

An hour later, Jovanna was up at the patch, scared, nervous and not knowing where to go but knowing that she couldn't go home. She'd never go back home. Several cars had approached her, but she shook all of them off.

The police made their gratuitous hourly trip through the Patch. She ducked back between two buildings. A skinny black girl no more than her age, was giving an old man a blow job while he smoked on a glass straight shooter.

As soon as the cops had passed, Jovanna stepped back out onto the street.

A big black Navigator pulled up in front of her. "Yo! Babygirl!"

She turned to see who was calling her.

"So he finally let you out, huh?"

"Who? What are you talking about?" she asked.

"Rice, that's who. I didn't think that he would ever let your tight pussy, good dick sucking, young ass out of his sight."

"Yeah, I thought that you had the nigga sprung," came the voice of the man in the passenger seat.

"Come on little mama and give us a chance to see what'chu all about?'

Jovanna thought to herself, *So, he's been talking about me to his friends. Is this what he wants me to be...a ho?* Taking a deep breath, she climbed into the big black truck.

Rice woke up to a dirty kitchen. She was really gone. He got up, cleaned the kitchen and bedroom, then headed over to kick it with his man, Cedric.

He knocked on the door. No one answered. He knocked again. The Navigator was parked in the drive. He was just about to leave when the door opened. Cedric and Scott were in the living room getting dressed. The door to the bedroom was closed, tight.

Rice stepped in to the living room talking loudly. "What's up, ma niggas? Man it feels good to be free. I kicked that young ho's ass out last night. Hell, she was fuckin' up my groove. Hogging all of this for herself." He grabbed a handful of crotch.

"What did y'all niggas do last night? Did you get your freak on?"

Ced and Scott remained silent and continued to get dressed.

"Oh, shit! I see! The freak is still here! She's in the bedroom! Who is it? Is it Brigette? Is it Sheka and some of her crew?"

Rice ran to the bedroom door and flung it open. Jovanna was just getting out of bed. Her hair, which was normally combed with every hair neatly in place, was matted to her head with cum. A thin white sheet was wrapped around her otherwise naked body. She held a fistful of big face bills.

Rice turned and ran out of the house, not once turning and looking back.

Chapter Twenty-Eight

I hadn't seen or heard from Geno in several days. Geno hadn't been to work and his wife had been calling every day, looking for him. This wasn't like Geno. He always went home at night. *Always.*

Freddy was helping out in the office as well as driving. He was clean for the most part. Having slipped several times in the past few years, he'd finally gotten back on the right track.

Brigette hadn't come back to see Tatiana. I was surprised by her not showing up. She seemed to be clean. And she definitely looked like she was clean. She looked damn good. Damn good. And something was fishy with Nae Nae. She was trying to fuck me to death. As soon as I would step through the door, she would jump me for a quickie fuck or a fast blow job. Whatever she was up to, it was working. I would cut work short, so I could hurry home to my horny wife.

It was 3:30 PM, and I was just about to head home when my cell phone rang.

"Hello."

"Chris, I don't know if you remember me or not. My name is Sheka, Brigette's friend. Um, I'm calling because she's at the Patch, and she's gonna smoke herself to death."

"But Sheka, what am I supposed to do? I can't make her stop."

"No, but maybe if she sees you, it'll make her *want* to stop. She's still in love with you, you know."

"Did she tell you that?"

"She didn't have to. I'm a woman too."

"So it's that obvious?" he asked.

"Yes, to another woman."

I took a deep breath. Nae Nae and Brigette had spent a lot of time together while I was in the hospital. Maybe Nae Nae said or did something that scared Brigette away.

"Look Sheka, I'm on my way up there. Does she know where you live?"

"Do you know where *your* pussy lives?"

"Are you always sarcastic?"

"Is your dick ever hard?"

She burst out laughing and hung up the phone.

I hollered out to Freddy who was cleaning out one of the black Towncars. The Hummer and stretch Escalade were out making money.

"I'm gone for the night Freddy. See you tomorrow." I pulled a freshly cleaned Lincoln out and hit the street, searching for Brigette. I went up Ontario Avenue to Tenth and turned right, hitting the Patch. Several girls were slowly strutting down both sides of the street, proudly displaying their God given attributes. Large tits, small waits and asses of every size and shape paraded around the Patch.

I pulled over and parked. A very young black girl with divine proportions wearing extremely short daisy dukes slowly walked past my car. Two attractive white girls and a tall extra pretty, light-skinned black girl strutted by. Old Karen walked by, smiling, waving. For a moment I wondered how things might have been had I married her instead of my first wife.

A patrol car cruised past. Both men looked over in my direction and smiled. Probably thought that I was out tricking. A knock on the window startled me. A young boy, no more than sixteen was trying to sell a bunch of old cassette tapes. He probably needed the money for more crack. I waved him away.

A game of 4-5-6 or ceelow began in front of a white front four suite apartment. Two young men wearing velour sweat-suits and wearing lots of gold went into the building. A half an hour later, they came out with their sweat shirts in their hands. One of them was sweating profusely. I got out of the car and approached the two young men.

"Yo! Where can a nigga go to get his freak on with some fine assed snowflake. You know something special."

Both niggas looked at each other, then exchanged high fives amid loud screams of laughter. "Yeah pops. If you can handle it, go up to apartment four," answered one of the men."

"But don't go if you've got a weak heart Pops. She's something else," said the second.

I nodded and quickly went over to the apartment and up the stairs. I straightened my tie and wiped my bald head before knocking on the door.

"Come on in. I'm in the shower. You can come and join me, or wait in the living room. Your choice." The voice came from inside the apartment. I opened the door and stepped in. I walked into the almost empty living room and sat down on the only piece of furniture in it, a pink sofa. I looked around the room. The paint was fresh, the linoleum used and a roach was crawling across the floor.

Brigette stepped out of the bathroom with a large towel barely covering the important parts and a towel wrapped around her head like a turban. She froze the moment she saw me.

"Hello, Brigette. How are you?"

"What are you doing here? What do you want?" She walked over to the door and opened it. "Will you please leave?"

"Not until we talk." I pushed the door shut and locked it.

"Chris, you and I have nothing to talk about. I'm sure that bitch of a wife of yours has already told you all that you needed to know."

"Nae? What's Nae got to do with this?'

"You mean she didn't show you?"

"Show me what? What's going on here?"

Brigette sat down on the pink sofa. She put her face in her hands and started to cry.

I sat down beside her. My arm went around her, comforting her.

"Brigette, your friend Sheka called me. She was concerned that you might be suicidal, that you've been smoking dope uncontrollably."

Brigette continued to cry. She leaned over resting her head on my chest. The towel that was covering her came a loose. Her bare breast burst out of the towel. Every time that she boohooed the towel would drop even more. I tried to tie the towel back around her tempting breast. I failed. Instead my hand brushed against her hardened cherry-sized nipple.

Brigette stopped crying momentarily and looked up at me. I looked down into her tear-filled, reddened eyes. I felt as if I was looking through her deep blue eyes and straight into her soul. I reached up and removed the towel from her head. Her long blonde tresses dropped down, resting on her shoulders. I leaned down, kissed a tear that rested on her cheek, and swallowed the salty taste. Brigette threw her arms around my neck and pulled me down with her, falling back on the sofa. Her towel had fallen completely away. She lay naked beneath me.

"Brigette, I can't. I'm married to Nae Nae. I'd love to, but I can't."

"So I'm not good enough for you. Is that it? I'm just a crack-smoking ho now, right? Too dirty for your precious dick?"

"Brigette stop. That's not it at all."

"That conniving assed bitch of a wife of yours ain't as fucking pristine clean as she appears to be. She walked right into this man's house and snapped pictures of us fucking like she's been there before."

"What? Nae Nae did what?"

"So she really didn't show you, huh?"

"Show me what? What the hell are you talking about? Start at the beginning, please."

"About a week ago, I met these two guys and went to trick with them. It was my first relapse in eighteen months. They were nice, and I'd met them before in Buffalo the day I came back. Well, we were just finishing up when Nae Nae burst in filming us with a DVD recorder."

"Nae Nae! *My* Nae Nae!!

"Yes, *your* fucking Nae Nae. Then she drops them a stack of money and leaves. Only one of them calls her sis. Does Nae Nae have a brother?"

"Uh, yeah, a half brother." I lied. *So Nae Nae was up to something. She set Brigette up to get rid of her. That's why she's been fucking my brains out. She's afraid of Brigette. Afraid that I'd fuck her. And who is this guy she calls her brother? She claimed that me and Otis are the only men that she's ever fucked.*

"Do you remember the house that you went to that night?" I asked.

"I sure do. It's a huge house on Park Place."

"Good, take me there later tonight."

"Later? Why not now?"

"'Cause I've got something better to do right now!"

I stood up and removed my tie. Brigette reached up and loosened my belt as I ran my fingers through her hair.

Chapter Twenty-Nine

Ashley and Amber hit a couple of real good licks. They'd amassed almost three hundred dollars. Not wanting to spend it all on crack and wanting to get the most of their money, they called up Janet and Janis, twin friends of theirs. Janet and Janis were eighteen years-old and extremely streetwise. Sometimes local dealers would sell them 8 balls for eighty bucks. A quick double-up. Ashley gave Janet $160. Janet went to see Stu, a long time acquaintance.

Stu had been trying his best to get into her pants, but Janet wasn't having it. She made it clear that no poo butt nigga was getting shit from her. If you wanted some ass from her, you'd better have plenty of cheddar. She walked up to knock on his door, but before she could knock the door opened.

"Well, well, well. What brings you to my crib? Are you in *need* of something?" Stu put a lot of emphasis on the word need.

"Cut the crap, Stu! This is business. I need a double up!" She pushed past him and stepped inside of his crib.

"Is that *all* that you want?" This time he emphasized all. Stu eyed Janet's ass as she walked past him wearing a pair of Polo jeans that were so tight that she had to lay flat on her bed in order to squeeze her fine ass into them. Stu went into his bedroom and plopped down on the bed. Reaching under the bed, he pulled out a shoe box half filled with large chunks of powder. He took one out and called to Janet, "Hey baby, you gonna have to wait for me to cook it up."

"Damn! Damn nigga, you ballin' like that?" *There must be at least a brick up in here?'*

Stu slid the box back up under the bed and sat up much too late. Janet had already seen it all.

"Come on nigga. Let a bitch in on the come up." Janet sat on the bed beside him. Her fingers played across the back of his white wife beater. "Stu, a bitch needs some cheddar. Me and Janis are trying to get to the Magic Show up in Vegas. We got our own fashion design that we want to present. My girl, Brigette gave me the idea. It's called *'The Strawberry Patch'* fashions by J&J Langston. But we'll need about $2,500 to get there and put us up for a week."

"So what you sayin' and I ain't got $2,500 yet anyway."

Janet's brain took off running. Powder equals crack which equals money. She turned on the charm.

Stu wasn't anybody's fool though. There wasn't a pussy in the world worth $2,500, not even hers. "So what 'chu got in mind, babygirl? How do you plan on making $2,500?" asked Stu.

"Well, I was thinking that maybe I can help you push this shit. You cook it up and front me like six ounces at a time and I-"

"Why should I help you? Why should I give a fuck about you, your sister, or your fuckin' clothes. Every time a nigga try to kick it wit'chu, you knock a nigga down!"

Janet stood up and put her hands on her sexy ass hips. "Look, you know that I don't like playing games. Spit out what'chu saying!"

"What I'm saying is that you play and I'll pay. But this is how it's going to be. I want $25,600 for the brick. There are thirty-two ounces here. That's only $800 an ounce. That's cheap as fuck, specially 'cause I'm frontin' the shit."

Janet smiled and asked, "Is that it?"

"'Course not. Since I'm taking a huge risk by frontin' you this shit, every five days you gotta come and kick it with a nigga until your bill is paid. Call it...*interest.*"

"So I give you some pussy and we've got a deal?"

"That's what I'm saying shorty. So what's it gonna be? Time's a wasting and I've got to cook all of this shit up."

Janet started rocking from side to side. She got to running through her head. She could pick up eight ounces on the blow up, sell 8 balls at $125, ounces at $850 times 40. Yes, she could come close to ten grand of her own money. It shouldn't take a month. She might have to fuck him, *maybe* five times...five times for a chance to make 10 G's.

"This is just between us, right?" she asked.

"Right."

"Then get your sorry ass up and get to cookin' partner. I need to see what we're working with."

Stu reached under the bed and grabbed the shoe box. Minutes later Stu was breaking off his first batch of crack. He sent Janet to the store to get six more boxes of Arm and Hammer baking soda. An hour later, he was done. They weighed up the crack, 1,176 grams.

"Damn nigga! You was a little light in the powder, wasn't you? This shit came back short didn't it?"

"Look bitch, you making me mad. Is it a deal or not? If it's a deal, get naked. If it ain't, get gone!"

"Calm down big nigga, calm down." Janet went into Stu's bedroom and sat on the edge of his bed. "Remember, just between us."

Stu pulled his wife beater up over his head and walked over, stopping directly in front of Janet.

She took a deep breath, kicked off her Filas and lay back on the bed. Two hours later, she was back on the Patch. Amber, Ashley and Janis were frantic.

"Damn Sis, where the fuck you been? These bitches were sweatin' the shit out of me. And why you change clothes and shower and shit?"

Janet gave the girls an 8 ball apiece. "I'm sorry that I took so long. If you girls need more, call us. Any time of day or night. In fact, let the hoes on the stroll know that we've got the Flav."

Janis looked at her sister. She didn't know what, but something was definitely different with her.

"Come on, Janis. I've got a lot to tell you." She grabbed her sister by the arm and led her down the Patch.

She started filling her sister in on all of the details of their deal, including the sex.

"Girl, no you didn't fuck that ugly assed nigga! I don't believe that you fucked him! Damn girl! Now I feel guilty."

"Good, then next time you can fuck that long dick bastard."

"Was he long?"

"Girl, he was all up a bitch's stomach and shit."

"I don't want to hear no more, girl."

"OK."

"How long was he?"

"Girl, forget it. We've got a lot of dope to move. The longer we take, the more pussy he gets. And one day he may want some ass."

"I don't want to think about it."

"Where's your phone?"

"I'm way ahead of you."

It was time to let the people of the Patch know that they were in business. It was time to Window Shop.

Chapter Thirty

Crack was flowing through the Patch like water. Everybody had some and it was all good. Every corner was packed with low level dealers. And everyday a new girl would show up on the stroll.

I was trying to get a hold of our babysitter, Lisa. I was going to take Nae out for awhile so that I could nail down what exactly she was up to.

"Hello, Lisa?"

A hardy laugh came over the phone. "No, this is Ted, Lisa's stepdad. May I ask who's calling?"

"Um, yes, this is Christopher Daniels. Lisa babysits for my wife and I. She should be expecting my call. Is she in?"

"Why no. She left here about ten minutes ago. Maybe she's on her way over there."

"Great. Sorry for bothering you."

"No bother at all. Nice talking to you."

"Bye."

Ted hung up the phone. He could hear the water running in the shower. A wicked smile crossed his face. He picked the phone back up and dialed seven digits.

"Hey baby, it's me Ted."

"Hi Sweetheart, what's up."

"I forgot to get an oil change and the tires rotated on the Focus. Would you be a dear and go to Jiffy Lube and get it taken care of for me? I'll even start dinner."

"Of course dear. I'll swing by as soon as I finish up at the grocery."

"See you when you get here. Bye." Ted hung up the phone and started up stairs. The running water had stopped. He followed the silence. There were three doors at the top of the stairs. Ted put his ear to the furthest. Clothes rustling.

Slowly he tried to turn the doorknob. Locked. He tiptoed back down the stairs, turned and ran back up them. He faked a trip at the top and fell all the way back down them, landing on the bottom landing.

"Ahhgg!! Help!! Ahhgg!!"

Lisa opened her door and ran down the stairs to see if Ted was Okay. She was in such a hurry that she hastily tied her robe around her and it had come undone as she ran down the stairs. A long, smooth, milk white thigh shone through the opened robe.

Ted reached out and grabbed her, pulling her down on top of him. He yanked the robe wide open. She was only wearing a pair of black panties. Lisa kicked and swung with all her might, but it only excited Ted more. He pulled the robe down over her shoulders and buried his head in her breast. His right hand held hers while his left hand went deep inside of her panties.

She screamed. Ted covered her mouth with is. She started to cry, but deep down she knew that crying would do her no good. She fought and kicked for as long as she could until fatigue caused her to submit.

Ted lifted her exhausted body up high enough to remove her panties. He stuck them under his nose and took in a deep breath, savoring the scent. He immediately became hard. He was naked in seconds.

"Little lady, I've been waiting a long time for this moment. It's Showtime!"

"Please don't. What about mom? What about my mother?"

Ted ignored her pleas. He lifted her naked body up onto the sofa. Her legs parted. Ted was in her. He moved slowly at first. Then he pounded her with all his might.

Lisa decided that it was futile to fight. She just lay there waiting for him to finish. She wasn't a virgin. In fact she'd had protected sex with several of her high school male friends. She'd even enjoyed it with a few.

But this was different. She didn't enjoy it. It wasn't right. He was her mother's husband, and had been so for the last ten years. Her mother worshipped the ground that he walked on. She truly loved him.

Lisa tried to make her mind go blank. Tried to erase the moment. Make it never happen. And then she felt him come deep inside of her. His seering hot fluid warmed her entire insides. He relaxed his whole body. All of his weight was on her. His soft shrinking dick sloshed as it squirted out of her.

Laura had forgotten her Visa card. It was lying on top of her dresser. She'd driven home and parked in front of the house since she was darting right back out. She opened the door to the living room and froze. Ted and Lisa both scrambling for their clothes.

Ted found his pants and jumped into them. He ran up to Laura. "Baby! I'm sorry. But I couldn't help myself. She's all the time flaunting and teasing me. Every time that you leave the house, she's flashing me a tit or something!"

Laura was speechless. *What had she done wrong? What had she done to deserve this. This was unthinkable.* Her eyes went up and down her beautiful daughter's body as she ran past her. She was hot. Even her mother had to admit that. But there were no bruises, no signs of force. She walked over and picked up the pair of black lace panties. No tears, no rips. They hadn't been torn off. Tears began to run down Laura's face. Something had to change. It was clear. The three of them could no longer live in the same house. One of them had to go.

Ted was on his knees in front of her holding her around both legs crying and ranting on and on about how Lisa bewitched him. Laura thought about how happy they'd been or so they seemed. And Ted was a wonderful husband and a good provider. She'd often received flowers and candy, sometimes for no reason at all, other than him loving her. Even the sex was good, slow, gentle, giving.

She wondered if he'd been as gentle with Lisa. Softly, she pushed Ted away and slowly started her long journey up the stairs.

Decisions, decisions, she thought as she climbed the long staircase.

Lisa was now fully dressed, laying across her bed crying.

Well, at least she's sorry for what she did. Somehow Laura felt that the whole thing was her fault. She kept blaming herself. Maybe she should have stayed with John, Lisa's *blood* father. He cheated a lot and drank even more, but at least *this* wouldn't have happened.

Laura sat on the edge of the bed and began to stroke her daughter's long black hair. Lisa threw her arms around her mother and wept aloud.

"I'm so sorry mom. I really am. But I couldn't stop him. I tried mama. I really tried, but I got so tired. I fought 'til I got tired mama!"

Laura helped her daughter up to a sitting position. She wiped away her tears. Their eyes locked.

"Do you forgive me, mama? Please! I have to know! Do you forgive me mama?" cried Lisa.

With snakelike bitterness Laura struck Lisa across her face with her opened hand. The sound resonated throughout the house.

"Get out of my house! Whore! How could you, you whore! Get out! Get out!" Laura was screaming at the top of her lungs.

Lisa jumped up off of the bed and ran out of the bedroom door, past a sniveling Ted. She flew down the stairs and out of the door. She ran and ran and ran. She had no idea where she was going. The tears stopped running on the outside, but they still flowed on the inside.

How could she choose him over me? I'm her own flesh and blood. Her only child. He raped me! He raped me! Lisa's mind was running faster than she could keep up with.

She needed to get away. To forget. She wanted to die. She reached into her jean pants pocket and pulled out a small wad of money. One hundred and thirty six dollars. No clothes, no place to stay and only one hundred and thirty six dollars to her name.

The Daniels. Maybe they'll help me, she thought. She hit Pine Avenue heading toward 19th. When she came to the McDonalds on 13th, she stopped in to get a bag of fries and a chocolate shake.

As soon as she opened the door to walk in, she heard someone calling her name. "Lisa! Lisa! It's us, Ashley and Amber. Damn it's good to see you girl! What's up?"

Lisa smiled. She was glad to see her friends. She needed someone to talk to that would understand. The three of them ate. Lisa footed the bill. Amber's eyes lit up when she saw Lisa's bank. Lisa spilled the story on them. They lapped it up like hungry pups.

"Come and hang with us. We move around a lot, but we look out for each other," stated Amber.

"Right, and we stays h-i-g-h!" laughed Ashley.

"I could use some get high right about now," said Lisa.

"All we've got is some rock. Wanna try it?"

"Why not? If it'll help me feel better, why the fuck not?"

The three girls left the McDonalds and headed back down to Tenth Street, heading to the Patch.

Laura was lying on the bed naked with her legs thrown high up on Ted's shoulders as he pounded away at her saliva soaked pussy. Her eyes closed. She thought back to her daughter. She wondered where she was, *was she alright? Where was she going to spend the night?* A moistened finger made its way up the crack of her wide ass. Ted grunted and began to pump like a horny dog on a bitch in heat.

"AAhhgg!" Ted's body trembled as he came. It shook and shook until he'd delivered every drop of cum deep inside of her. Then he relaxed, letting all of his body weight drop down on top of her.

She wrapped her arms around him and held him tight. This was the way she wanted it to be. Her and her man. She felt that she deserved it.

Chapter Thirty-One

Jennifer, Tynesha, Sharon and Jill had just gotten out of Niagara County Jail. They'd spent most of the summer locked down. Now they were fresh, fiening and ready to do whatever was necessary to get high. One of their steady tricks, old man Charlie, had come to pick them up in his Blue Ford Explorer. As soon as they ran out to him, they shouted,

"Hey Mr. Charlie! Are we glad to see you! Can we go back to your place?" shouted Sharon.

"For what? So that you can cry about how long he lasts?" laughed Jill.

"Or how big he is," added Jennifer.

Mr. Charlie opened the door and loaded the girls in. Then they headed back to the Falls.

"Mr. Charlie, can we stop somewhere and get us a blast?" asked Jennifer as she stroked his thigh. Every now and then letting her fingers run down into the middle of the old man's crotch.

"No, we've got to go to my house so you girls can get cleaned up. Some friends of mine are having a party and I've got you girls hooked up to attend."

"Party? What kind of party?" asked Jill.

"Your kind of party. Lots of men, lots of money and lots of drugs," answered the older gentleman.

"Who's giving it?" asked Tynesha.

"Does it matter?"

Tynesha paused and looked down at the floor. She'd stopped smoking crack and was secretly going to those N.A. meetings. She'd even started seeing a young man there. At least she did before she went to jail. But it was hard for her since all of her friends smoked rock and they did whatever it took to get it. That's how she ended up getting locked down. They were picked up by four undercover cops passing as tricks. When they got into the hotel room and started talking prices, the men flashed their badges and arrested them. That was ninety days ago. And now she was heading back to the same kind of life.

Mr. Charlie pulled into the alley behind his house and parked. All of the girls hurried into the big four bedroom house and ran upstairs to the bathroom to shower and get dressed. Except Tynesha.

"What's wrong, babygirl?" he asked.

"I'm just not feeling it tonight. That's all."

"Tynesha, I know what's going on. If you want to go see him first, then meet the girls there later. I'll explain things to them."

"But you'll be short a girl."

"I'll find one. I'll call Sheka."

Tynesha threw her arms around Mr. Charlie's neck and kissed him on top of his freshly shaved head.

"Thank you, Mr. Charlie! Thank you lots!" she cried as she ran upstairs to shower and dress. Mr. Charlie came up behind her. Tynesha ran on into the bathroom. Mr. Charlie stopped and opened the door to the first bedroom. Inside, his eighteen year old son, Charlie Jr., and several of his friends sat around playing Nintendo games.

"Hey Mr. Charlie, you going out with the girls tonight?" asked Everett, a skinny lanky light-skinned kid.

"No, I wasn't invited. And it's invitation only."

"Hey Dad, Nick and Everett and them say that you're a pimp. In high school, you're a legend for kickin' it to so many fine girls.

"I was showing them some of your pictures and some of them got mad 'cause their aunts and cousins were in there. Haa, Haa, Haa!" Charlie Jr. burst out laughing.

It was true. Over the past few years dozens of young runaway and confused girls had come to live with Mr. Charlie, trading sex and companionship for food, shelter and protection from the abusive young men of the hood. Often they would take pictures that he would hang on his wall. The pictures now covered one and a half of his bedroom walls.

"Charles, I've told you to stay out of my room! Those pictures are mine, not the public's. Some of those girls have gone and made good with their lives. Some have even gotten married. There's no sense in stirring sour milk, ya hear?"

Reluctantly, Charles Jr. answered, "Yes, dad, I hear."

Mr. Charlie backed out of the room and opened the next bedroom door. Tynesha sat on the edge of the bed, naked, drying herself with a large pink bath towel. He closed the door, walked across the hall and opened a third bedroom door. Sharon, Jennifer and Jill were in different phases of undress.

"We're almost ready, Mr. Charlie," stated Jennifer, never stopping her movements of getting dressed. No signs of embarrassment from any of them.

Mr. Charlie closed the door and stepped in. "You girls probably won't be back 'til morning," he stated.

"Did you need something before we left, Mr. Charlie?" asked Sharon as she slid into a red patent leather skirt. The skirt barely made it up over her wide hips. She sucked in her stomach so that she could zip it up.

He lay down on the bed, flat on his back. Sharon walked over, unbuckled his pants and pulled out his semi-hard dick. She went about giving the old man head. The other girls kept right on getting dressed as if the action on the bed was the most natural, normal thing on earth.

Jennifer was the first girl completely dressed. She walked over and tapped the tiring Sharon on the shoulder. "Move girl. Go finish getting dressed."

Sharon got up and Jennifer took her place. Within seconds she had Mr. Charlie shooting his load into her warm, wet mouth.

Jill was there in an instant with a hot wet towel. She cleaned Mr. Charlie's soft dick and groin area while Jennifer went to deposit his cum into the toilet and brush her teeth. Soon they were loaded into the Explorer and on their way to the party. He dropped everyone off except for Tynesha.

"What's up Tynesha? Ain't you coming?" asked Jennifer. The two other girls were curious as well.

"Before Tynesha could answer, Mr. Charlie blurted out, "She's going with me. We have another more pressing engagement."

"Well alright girl! Are you gon' meet us there later?" Sharon asked.

"Yea, I'll be there as soon as I can."

With the other girls gone, Tynesha looked over at the old man and said, "Thank you, Mr. Charlie. I owe you one."

"No, you don't owe me shit! You go do you. That's all I ask of you. Be yourselves and do you."

He went over to the soup kitchen on Falls Street. People were standing in front of the building, smoking cigarettes and talking shit with each other.

Tynesha froze up. "Mr. Charlie, I'm scared. I don't know what to tell him. Where can I say that I've been? What if he doesn't believe me? I can't tell him that I've been tricking the last two years, can I?"

Mr. Charlie parked the truck and shut off the engine. He climbed out, walked around and opened the door for her. He held out his hand. "Come on Tynesha. I'll go with you."

She put her hand in his and he lead her into the meeting. As soon as they stepped in, a light-skinned young man, maybe twenty-five years old, came over to greet them.

"Tynesha! How have you been? Where have you been? Is everything alright?"

Mr. Charlie could tell by the gleam in the young man's eyes that this was the young man that Tynesha had spoken of.

"Everything is fine now son. We had some family issues that had to be resolved. But that's done now. She's here to stay now, for as long as she wishes." Mr. Charlie shook the young man's hand and kissed Tynesha on the cheek.

"Thank you, Mr. Charlie! Thank you very much!" said Tynesha as her and her young companion took seats in the front row.

Mr. Charlie got back into his truck and drove home. The boys were still in Charlie Jr.'s room playing video games. The girls were at the party. The men were pleased with what they'd seen. They explained that Tynesha would join them later. Jennifer collected $600, the amount they'd greed on, $150 each.

The N.A. meeting was over. Tynesha agreed to go out for coffee with her male friend. She'd catch up with the girls another time.

Black, Cleve and T-Bone had set out the weed, the Hennessey and the powder cocaine. Steve was outside in the backyard, playing with Bruno.

Chapter Thirty-Two

I took Brigette by the house on Park Avenue so that she could show me the house where Nae Nae's supposedly brother lived. Then we went by the limo shop and I showed her the DVD of Tiffany and the dog, Bruno.

Brigette cried all the way through it. She told me what was going to happen before it was shown on the screen. When Tiffany stopped moving, Brigette explained that she had died. She must've suffocated on the sock that they had stuffed in her mouth to quiet her. Now they knew who her killers were, the four men that were in the video.

"You know I saw her the night she died."

"I know. She told me."

"She told you? But how?"

"I was talking to her on the phone when the men burst in. I heard everything. *Everything*!"

"Should we go to the police?"

"I don't know. Is this enough to convict those bastards?"

"It is for me." I removed the DVD and popped another one in the DVD player. Several white girls and a light-skinned black girl were being positioned over upturned chairs, their asses in the air. The same large pit bull that fucked Tiffany was lead out and up on each of the girl's upturned naked behinds. The girls were still, extremely still. Chris wondered if they were drugged. He shut off the DVD player and removed that DVD too.

"I've seen enough. I'm going to the police. This ain't right. It just ain't right. They killed Tiffany and now they're raping sick young women with a fucking dog," I screamed as I helped Brigette out of the Hummer.

"I'm going with you!"

"Well come on. I'll deal with Nae and her friends later."

We jumped into one of the black Towncars and headed to the Niagara Falls Police Station...

• • •

Steve was busy crushing the Rohypinol pills into powder so that it could be mixed with the powder cocaine. Rohypinol or *roofies*, as they were called, was popular in the 90's as the date rape drug.

Jennifer and Sharon had stripped down to their panties and bras as they danced with each other. Jill had taken a medium sized cucumber from out of the refrigerator and had inserted half of it deep inside of her to the amazement of the men that were sitting around them.

Black was in his bedroom setting up the DVD camcorder. "Yes bitches, first me and my crew are gonna fuck the shit out of ya'll then I get my money back from you, and then I throw your whorish asses to the dogs. *Literally*!" He laughed aloud as he went about his business.

"All right girls! Here's the nose candy! Everybody snort up! We're about to begin the party!" Steve set the powder on the coffee table beside Sharon and Jennifer. Both girls took long thick lines up their noses. Jill followed.

"Hey girls! Where's the other chick? The one that's usually with y'all?" asked Steve as he took off his shoes and socks then his shirt.

"She should be here any minute now," answered Jennifer. She took in another thick line of powder. "Damn this is some potent shit. I can hardly move my arms!" shouted Sharon as she tried to dance.

Jill was snorting as much as her thick ass could handle. She pulled the cucumber out from between her legs and bit off the end of it. She tried to chew it but couldn't. Pieces of it dribbled out of the sides of her mouth. She could sense that something was wrong. By now both Jennifer and Sharon had become incapacitated also. T-Bone and Cleve removed the rest of the girls clothing.

Cleve looked down at Sharon's near perfect body and said, "Damn niggas, I gots to have me some of this fine ass ho."

He pulled off his pants, got on top of her and began to pump away. Black hopped on Jennifer and followed suit. He played with her big breasts as he pounded her small framed body.

T-Bone walked over to Jill and flipped her over onto her stomach. "Shit, after taking that fat assed cucumber up her pussy, my dick ain't gone do shit. I'll take some of her ass instead." He began to punish Jill's tight pink bottom.

Someone knocked at his door. Steve went over and looked through the peep hole. A very attractive young lady stood at the door. "Who is it?" he asked.

"It's Tynesha. Is Jennifer and them still here?"

Steve looked around at his crew members banging away at the drugged girls' pussies and ass. It made him horny.

He cut off the lights and let her in. The sounds of fucking could distinctly be heard. "Come on in. They've already started. Jennifer has the money."

Steve led Tynesha to the back bedroom. He closed the door behind them and cut on the light. "Damn, babygirl, I had no idea you was this fine. You're fine. Fine, fine, fine,

fine. In fact, where's your daddy?" He laughed out loud at his own joke.

She burst out laughing. She'd heard Richard Pryor's album too. She blushed and said, "Thank you. You're funny."

It was Steve's turn to blush. "You're alright Tynesha. I like you. You're really cool to be a h-"

Tynesha dropped her head.

"I'm sorry. I didn't mean to call you a h-"

"Maybe I should go.'

"No, please don't go. Please don't go." Steve led her to the huge king sized pillow top bead. They sat on the edge of the bed and talked...

• • •

The police reviewed the DVD and I.D'd two of the men, Cleveland Simms and Stewart Brach, both low level drug dealers with extensive records. Sergeant Steffi was a mountain of a man. He stood 6'2" and weighed over 330 pounds. His shoulders were over 3 feet wide.

"We'll send a car out to look for them first thing in the morning. They won't be hard to find. Do you mind leaving these with us?" he said as he held up the two DVDs. I shook my head no.

Brigette and I shook the lieutenant's hand and left, confident that we'd done all that we could as far as catching those scumbags. We rode around talking about past times. We laughed through some parts, and we cried through others. The night ended when we pulled up in front of Brigette's apartment.

"I'd better go home. It's late," I sadly admitted.

Brigette leaned over and kissed me on the cheek. "I know... It's been nice though." She opened the door and stepped out of the car.

"Brigette!"

"Yes, Chris?" she answered as she bent down. She was looking me straight in the eyes.

"Have a safe night."

"You too," she sighed as she closed the car door and stepped away.

I watched as she walked up the stairway to her tiny apartment. Once she was out of sight, I pulled off and headed home.

On my way home my mind ran in a variety of directions- *Tiffany's brutal murder, Brigette's crack filled life, and my wife's cunning interference with me and Brigette's relationship. And who was this supposed to be brother of hers?*

I parked the car and looked at my watch, 1:30 AM. I walked quietly up the stairs. My bedroom door was cracked open. As soon as I pushed the door open, little Jessica ran over and jumped into my arms.

"Daddy, Daddy, you finally got home." She wrapped her little arms around me and squeezed me tight.

"I love you daddy."

"I love you too baby." I carried her back over to our bed and lay her down next to her mother. Nae Nae woke up.

"Hi Chris. What time is it?" she asked rubbing her eyes.

"It's late. Go back to sleep. But wake me before you leave for work in the morning, OK?"

"Sure baby. Is something wrong?"

"No baby, there's just something that needs to be done before you go to work."

"OK, Goodnight. I love you."

"I know baby. I know!"

Nae closed her eyes. But she couldn't sleep wondering what I was up to. She lay there thinking as she listened to me as I showered.

Chapter Thirty-Three

Cedric, Scott, Cobbs and Rice were sitting on Highland Avenue smoking a blunt and sipping Henny, watching the happenings down in the hood. Rice had gotten over the fact that his boys had fucked Jovanna. It hurt at first, but hell, her true colors had come through, that's all. He couldn't let himself get emotionally involved with a ho. Never that!

"Hey! Ain't that them twins? Janet and Janice. They sure been on the set a lot here lately. They pushin' more shit than we are," explained Cobbs.

"Yeah, I wonder who's frontin' them? Who they fuckin'? I thought they were dykes, but getting' all that dope. They're fuckin' somebody," shot Scott.

Cedric hit the blunt and slowly exhaled. Then he took a sip of Henney from his cup. It burned as it went down his throat. He stared at the girls. "Y'all might have a point. They did blow up fast. Damn, they just hit off Jessie Dell. Jess always cops an ounce or more. Damn, I'm like y'all. Who is these bitches fuckin'?"

They sat there and watched as the girls hit lick after lick after lick. Rice hopped out and served a few of their own customers. Crackhead Nina sped by. She was still walking at 100 miles per hour and was still wearing her red New York baseball cap. The nice ass that she once had was now flat as hell, and her breasts were undetectable under the loose fitting grey sweat shirt that she wore.

"Hey, ain't that old Karen?" shouted Scott

"Damn! It sure is! She's looking good," answered Cobbs.

"Yeah, I hear she's all cleaned up and getting married."

"No shit! Who she marrying?"

"Some dude with a little paper. Been working at the Dupont plant on Buffalo Avenue over thirty years. Heard they been fucking all that time."

"A trick marrying a ho! That'll never last."

"Naw man, he wasn't no trick. They were free recking. A real relationship type shit."

"Good for her. Karen was always a good girl. Good for her." Cedric started up the truck and got ready to pull off when Jovanna ran across in front of them.

"Damn!" They all said in unison. She was wearing a pair of white stretch pants that couldn't have been tighter. Her white blouse was tied above her navel which pushed her breasts up high. Her hair and face were impeccably done.

"Yo! Shorty!" Rice called out to her and ran over to catch up with her. Once he was face to face with her a warming sensation started in his feet then rose to engulf him.

She turned to face him. "How are you doing Rice?"

Hearing her call him Rice hurt him. She'd never called him Rice before. It was always honey, baby or boo.

"I'm doing alright," he lied. "How are you?"

"Do you really want to know? Should you check with your boys first. I don't want to cause any problems."

"Shorty, not right now. I came over to see if you were alright. Not to fight."

"Well thank you, but I'm fine. Just fine. Fucked up, insecure, neurotic, and emotional. So, if you don't mind, I'll talk to you later. Bye." She turned and strode away. She hadn't gone far when a bone colored Lexus rode up on her.

Rice turned his head, when he looked back, she was gone.

"Damn son, she cut your shit short as Cobbs' dick," laughed Scott.

"Why my dick gotta be short? Why I even gotta be in the conversation? This is supposed to be a time of jollification, not one of evisceration."

"Damn Cobbs, will you stop with the Don King shit and speak English?"

"I'm just trying to help my black brothers expand their vocabularies. I try to learn at least one word a day."

"Well, I'm gonna give you four words for the day. Shut, the, fuck, up! You got it. Shut, the, fuck, up!" said Cedric as he pulled doff.

Rice quietly sat on the passenger side as they rode down through the hood. They went down about six blocks and u-turned in the middle of the street. When they got back up to Highland and Fairfield, their original hang out, they saw the twins hop up into a red Ford Focus.

"Follow that bitch! Let's see who's frontin' these bitches." Shouted Rice.

Cedric stepped on the gas, pursuing the duo from a distance. The girls rode down Lewistown Road, then back up College Avenue to Highland.

"These bitches are trying to make sure that nobody's following them,"

"Well stay with them. Don't let them lose us."

They went through the Mounteagle Estates apartment complex and came out the Hyde Park side then turned back down toward Lewiston Road to McKoon. The girls parked in Stu's drive. It was time to make another payment and give Stu another shot of sex. They'd agreed to let him decide which one of them that he wanted.

The red Escalade stopped at the corner of McKoon. "That's Stu's house! Where the fuck is Stu getting enough dope to front these itches?" asked Cobbs.

"Maybe they supply him?" said Scott as he tried to make sense of the situation.

"I don't think so, it's almost 3:00 AM. If they supplied him, he'd be going to *their* house to cop, not vice versa." Cedric made a lot of sense, as always. They sat their quietly waiting to see what would happen next...

• • •

Tynesha had bad vibes about what was going on at the party. The living room was too quiet. Then the music was too loud. And she thought she heard a dog barking. She knew that something wasn't right.

Steve set the CD cover filled with powder in front of her. She politely refused. She was going to give that sobriety thing a try.

"Come on baby, it's free. This is on big Steve, baby. When you refuse, you make me feel stupid for offering."

"I'm sorry Steve, but I'm just not feeling this. Let me go get your money from Jennifer, so I can give it back to you."

She got up and headed toward the bedroom door. She tried to turn the knob, but it was locked.

"Steve, would you unlock the door?"

"Not yet babygirl. I'll unlock the door when they tell me to. Besides, I've got to have some of your fine ass."

Steve grabbed Tynesha and threw her on the bed, then dove on top of her.

The moment that her back hit the bed, she knew that she wasn't going to be able to leave that room without fucking the hulking man. "OK, OK!" she screamed. Her arms instinctively went up between them, separating his pounding chest from her soft breast. "Can I pee first? I don't want to wet the bed." She took a deep breath. "Please?" she pleaded.

Steve eased himself up off of her, never taking his eyes away from her. His eyes followed her all the way over to the door of the bathroom that set inside the huge master bedroom.

She stepped inside pulling the door shut behind her.

"No, No, No! sweetie. Leave the door cracked. And no funny stuff, ya hear."

Tynesha cracked the door, sat on the commode and began to trickle into the toilet. She pulled out the cell phone that she'd lifted from Steve. Quickly her nervous fingers danced across the keys.

"Hello, hello?"

She was afraid to answer.

Steve called out to her. "Don't make me have to come and get you! Wipe that thang off and bring it back in here. My dick is waiting!"

She set the phone down and flushed the toilet.

"Hello? Who is this? Jennifer? Tynesha?" Still Mr. Charlie got no answer. He closed his eyes, trying to imagine which one of his girls had called him. He strained to hear what was going on, on the other side.

Once the noise from the swirling toilet subsided, he thought that he could hear crying. "Tynesha!"

He hung up the phone and looked at the number. 990-7701. Bursting into Charlie Jr's room, he cut on the light. Charlie Jr., Everett, and Nick each had nice looking, young white girls writhering up under them. Everyone froze. The girls began to giggle.

"Charles, do any of you recognize this phone number? 990-7701?"

"Naw dad, it don't sound like any number that I know."

"What was that number again?" asked Amber, one of the three white girls.

"990-7701"

"That's crazy Steve's number, ain't it Andrea?" Lydia snuggled closer to Everett. "Y'all know that's his number."

"Who the hell is crazy Steve and where the fuck does he live?"

Andrea sat up, having to grab the comforter back up around her exposed breasts. The act was more one of respect for Mr. Charlie than out of embarrassment. "He lives with his mother up on 60th Street, but he always hangs out with Black and his crew over on Elmwood."

"Elmwood! I dropped the girls off on Elmwood. What's the address there?"

"I don't know the address, but it's a black and white bungalow."

Mr. Charlie turned and walked out of the room, closing the door behind him. He picked up his house phone and dialed a number.

"Hello?"

"What's up Renfro? It's me, Charlie."

"What time is it Charlie?"

"It's 3:00 AM. Time to go hunting. Call Marv, Frog, and the boys. I need y'all here in twenty minutes."

"What are we hunting for?"

"I'm not sure yet, but it's probably big."

He hung up the phone and went to his bedroom chest. Sitting in the corner was a loaded 12-gauge pump shotgun. He picked it up along with a bag of shells from off of the floor. Then he went outside to wait.

Chapter Thirty-Four

Nae Nae awakened me with her warm wet mouth on my rock hard penis. I responded by moving my hips to help her get better access. Her left hand began to softly knead my balls. Her touch was electric. Lighting every inch of my skin.

Damn! She felt good! Better than she'd ever felt before. My balls began to swell. She slid my dick out of her mouth and climbed up onto my chest. She slid a soft caramel thigh on either side of my head. My eyes still closed, the pungent scent of her womanhood stung my nose. Opening my eyes, I took in a long deep breath. Her smell excited me even more.

Opening my mouth as wide as I could, I kissed and sucked at her clit. I was rewarded with gyrations of her hips and moans that escaped her lips. My tongue led and her clit followed. They danced their own private dance. I continued until her body shook in orgasmic splendor.

I gently pulled her back and down. I entered her roughly. She shrieked! Her pussy was tight and warm. With each stroke she seemed to get tighter and tighter, and warmer and warmer. I continued to beat on her pussy with my big black fuck stick.

Nae Nae came again, grabbing hold of the cheeks of my ass and pulling them apart. She bucked hard and fast knocking my long hard dick out of her wetness. She got up on her hands and knees, offering me her tight asshole.

"Are you sure?" I asked, remembering the last time that we'd had anal sex. She was so sore that she had to lie on her stomach for two whole days. And now she was inviting me. *What's up?* I thought. I eased up behind her and slowly fed my saliva slickered dick into her hot tight bottom. I came quickly, spilling myself deep inside of her super stretched rectum

We fell over on our sides. My arms were still around her, and my dick was still up in her. I pulled her closer. She wiggled her ass.

"I love you Chris," she whispered.

"I love you too, baby!"

My mind drifted to me and Brigette and what we'd done earlier in the day. It was good what we'd done- maybe even great! But this! This thing with me and my lovely wife. This was perfection! Guilt set in. *How could I have been so stupid? How could I put my marriage in jeopardy for a fucking whore?*

Nae Nae moved her ass a little and my limp dick popped out. She snuggled even closer. Thoughts of Nae Nae leaving me and taking the kids with her entered my mind. I cared about Brigette, but I'd come to love my wife. I'd miss Brigette if she were to leave again, but I'd die if Nae were to leave. No one else on this earth could make me feel the way that I felt right then. With Nae in my arms, I was full, complete. Without her, well, I didn't even want to think about it.

We slept that way, naked and in each other's arms...

• • •

An old blue Chevy pickup with a white cap on the back pulled up. Mr. Charlie walked out and climbed into the passenger side.

"What's up Charlie?"

"22nd and Elmwood...middle of the block...a little black and white house."

"I know the place...Heavy on drugs...light on common sense... young black dudes," said Renfro.

Charlie was silent.

They pulled up two houses down from the little black and white bungalow. Charlie stepped out of the truck and motioned to Micky, Paul and Pete who followed them in Micky's black Suburban, to stop and wait. Charlie pulled the loaded shotgun off of the floor of the truck and headed toward the house. He crept up to the front of the house and peeked through the window.

Jennifer, Jill and Sharon were dressed, lying on the floor. None of them moved. He looked around for Tynesha. He didn't see her. He slid around to the back door and pressed his ear to the door. Nothing. He went to the bedroom window. The sound of a loud slap stopped him.

"Now see? See what you made me do? All you had to do was top fighting me. You ain't going no place until I fuck that fatty ass of yours."

Steve raised the long 4-inch wide belt and brought it across Tynesha's bare back. Her clothes were torn into several pieces. Literally torn away from her body.

Steve had raped her twice, but he wanted more. He wanted Tynesha's virgin ass. The one thing that she'd saved for marriage. And she just wasn't giving it up. Steve had worked himself into a frenzy. He began to beat her mercilessly with his huge fist. She cowered and tried to protect herself as best she could.

Charlie motioned to his friends to come to his aid. Renfro hopped out from under the wheel and opened the door to the cap. Marv, Ricardo, Sam, Tabor and Brooks all hopped out with a wide variety of weapons. A semi automatic 30-30, a double ot six, and two more 12-gauge shotguns loaded with deer shot.

Charlie went back around to the rear of the house and made a birdcall. Renfro answered with a birdcall of his own. Tabor and Brooks went to the front window. Renfro and Marv went to the front door while Ricardo slid around back with Charlie.

Steve had tied Tynesha's hands to the headboard and had just greased up his dick when Charlie knocked on the back door.

"Go away. Get the fuck away from my door if you know what's good for you!" screamed Steve.

Charlie knocked again, even harder.

"Look nigga! You asked for it!"

Steve pulled his pants on and picked his pistol up from under the bed. He stormed to the door. He unlocked it and swung it open.

Charlie stuck the long cold barrel of his shotgun in Steve's face. Ricardo relieved him of his handgun. They backed him into the bedroom.

"Say one word and I'll splatter your face," whispered Charlie. Once inside the room, Ricardo put the pistol to Steve's head while Charlie untied Tynesha's and wrapped a blanket around her. He whispered into her ear, "Go out to Uncle Micky's Suburban. Tell them to wait 'til the other girls come out, then tell them to take you back to my house. Everything is going to be alright now. I promise."

Tynesha wrapped herself up and ran out of the back door. They gagged and tied Steve up, then went into the hall, through the kitchen and up to the living room threshold.

Bruno began to bark furiously. Black released his hold on Bruno's leash. Bruno ran straight toward Ricardo who dropped him with a single shot to the head.

Black, T-Bone and Cleve jumped up scattering for their guns. Tabor and Brooks knocked out the front window and stuck the barrels of their weapons into the semi-darkened room. Renfro and Marv blew the front door off its hinges and ran in. Charlie and Ricardo ran in screaming, "Get your hands up! Get your fucking hands up!"

The boys froze and threw up their hands. The girls were beginning to stir. Marv, Renfro and Ricardo gagged and tied up the three boys while Brooks and Tabor helped the girls out to the Suburban.

Charlie went through the bound men's pockets gathering several thousand dollars. Charlie nodded and said, "Thank you. The girls have earned this." He turned and walked toward the door then stopped and said, "And oh, if you ever fuck with my girls again, or for that matter, anyone else associated with me, I'll kill you! And that's a promise!"

They quietly left the house and loaded back into the old blue pickup. It quietly sped away.

• • •

"They're gone whoever they were."

"Well come on, let's look inside. Maybe they've got the tapes."

"I'm scared."

"Well, I'm not!"

The door to the red Escort slammed shut. The four occupants went inside. One was brandishing a chrome plated .32 automatic.

Stu had been hiding in the half bath off of the kitchen. When everything was quiet, he decided to step out. His gun was in the living room with the rest of them. It was Black's policy to collect their guns and return them when they left. He stepped over the dead pit bull and walked into the living room at the exact moment that the four intruders stepped in.

"Don't shoot me! Please don't shoot me!" cried Stu who dropped to his knees and raised his arms high above his head, like a bitch.

"Where are the tapes?"

"Tapes? What tapes?"

"The tapes of us and the dogs."

"Oh, Ooh those tapes. They're in that box on the side of the television."

One of the intruders walked over and picked up the box of DVD's and tapes. As they turned to carry the box out, they accidentally knocked something to the floor.

"What's this? A camcorder!" She picked it up and turned it on. Three young ladies were knocked out, and a large pit bull was having his way with them. She turned it off. Tears began to build in her eyes. She tried to wipe them away. "Bastards!" She backed up, tripping over the coffee table, falling and spilling the contents of her purse. Lipstick, mascara, Newports, a 2-inch diameter, and an electric curling iron. She began gathering up her things and stuffing them back into her purse.

All Patsy thought about was killing the men that had raped her with a dog. All of that anger had hit a climax. She walked over to Black, put the gun to his head and pulled the trigger. Bloom! She handed the gun to Teri.

Teri walked over and put the gun to the back of Cleve's head. *BAM!* The slug went through the back of his head and came out of his eye, pulling the eye out of its socket. Teri handed the gun to Tara.

Tara's hand shook. It shook so bad that she almost dropped the gun. A huge hand grabbed and steadied her arm.

"Stokes here. Stokes will always be there to help his friends." Stokes helped her press the gun up against T-Bone's head. Tara closed her eyes...and pulled the trigger. *BAM, BAM!* Two shots to the head and T-Bone was dead.

Stu knew that he was next. He jumped to his feet to run, but he tripped over the dead pit bull that lay on the carpet before him. Stokes grabbed him by his ankle and dragged him back in front of the ladies. Tara handed him the gun. It was his turn now. He grabbed Stu by his huge Afro and popped two to his big water head. *Bong, Bong!*

Steve was still in the bedroom squirming as hard as he could try to get loose. As strong as he was he couldn't break free. His wrist began to bleed from the rope cutting into his arms from the pressure he was applying trying to break free.

He gave it one more try. This time the rope snapped, freeing his hands. He pulled so hard that one of his hands hit the lamp on the nightstand, knocking it over.

"What was that?" asked a nervous Tara.

"Somebody's in that back bedroom," answered Teri.

Stokes calmly walked over to the door, still holding the silver .32 automatic at his side. He eased the door open and saw the naked man, sitting on the edge of the bed trying to untie his feet.

Stokes ran over and grabbed Steve. Both men started to fight. The three girls ran in, watching the two men fight. Steve was a strong man, but his feet were bound and his wrists were sore and bleeding. Eventually Stokes overpowered Steve, holding him on the floor. Suddeny Stokes went crazy. "You!! You!! You!!" He screamed was he began to pound on Steve's head. Steve tried to cover his head, but Stokes knocked Steve out. Patsy and the girls had never seen Stokes filled with so much rage. It scared them.

Finally Stokes stopped his assault. He grabbed a sheet off the bed and began ripping the sheets into shreds. He then began tying Steve's hands behind his back. Once Steve's hands were bound, the big man handed Patsy the gun and took her purse off of her shoulder.

He fumbled around inside of it until he found what he was looking for, her electric curling iron. Stokes rolled Steve over, nearer to the electric outlet. He then forced the curling iron up Steve's hairy asshole. He spit on Steve as he plugged the cord into the outlet. As the curling iron began to heat up, Steve began to jerk rapidly, trying to squeeze the burning curlers out of his sizzling ass.

Stokes began to kick and stomp Steve's head. *Crack!* Steve's jaw broke. Blood began to pour out of his opened mouth. Stokes continued to stomp and kick the writhering man. Smoke began to rise up from Steve's ass. A strong stench filled the air. The girls turned their heads and covered their noses. Stove continued to stomp. He stomped until Steve stopped moving. Blood covered Stoke's shoes.

When Tara looked back at Steve she puked, her stomach retching over and over until there was nothing left to bring up. Stokes was standing over what used to be a man's head. Blood, skin, bone, and a grey gelationous matter lay there instead.

Tara grabbed Stokes by the arm and led him away. Police sirens roared in the background. Stokes stopped when they were all in the living room and slowly raised his shirt.

Scratches. Just like the ones that they had. Nothing was said until they were all at the car. Stokes stopped at the curb as the girls got in their car.

"Come on Stokes, get in. The police are coming," pleaded Tara.

"Stokes OK. Stokes be alright. You go ahead. Stokes will find you later."

"Are you sure?" asked Patsy.

"Stokes sure. You girls go. Go now!"

Stokes turned and pretended to walk away. As soon as the girls pulled off, Stokes ran back into the house.

Chapter Thirty-Five

It was 5:00 AM and Stu still hadn't come home. The girls had fallen asleep in the car, so had Cobbs, Rice and Scott. Cedric was still awake but barely. Rice's cell phone rang, waking everybody. He jumped up and wiped his eyes with both hands before answering it. The caller ID said *Out of Area.*

"Hello?"

"Hello Rice. You don't know me. I got your number from Geno. Geno's no longer with us, knowa-I-mean. So it's best to forget that you ever knew him, knowa-I-mean!" *Click*

"Yo Rice, who the fuck calling you at this time of the morning. A lick? A trick? J-O-V-A-N-N-A?" teased a sleepy-eyed Scott.

Rice thought for a minute. "Ugh, yeah. It was Jovanna. She still wants some of the rice man!"

They all laughed.

The girl's car started up and pulled away. The guys continued after them. The girls went to Cedric Court, one of the oldest projects in town. They parked and went into apartment E-6.

"That's where their mother lives. They must be in for awhile. Their moms don't play. They ain't gon' be runnin' in and out on her." Scott was looking at Cobbs as he spoke watching for a response.

Cobbs smiled. "Your choice of words leaves a lot to be desired. We, young intelligent black men, should help each other where our communication skills are concerned."

"Cobbs, not right now! We still don't know what's gong on with the twins and Stu. That's what we young intelligent black men need to be finding out! We can work on our communication skills later," barked Cedric as he pulled off heading home.

Police sirens screamed all through the hood. Several police cars were already parked in front of the tiny black and white house in the middle of the block on Elmwood. Two officers, a man and a woman, ran out the back door retching their insides off. What was once a man's head was now a pulverized mass of flesh, bone, and a grey gelatinous matter, splattered with blood.

Television crews began to arrive and set up their remote trucks with sound and picture. News reporters pulled up and parked in the drive behind the big black Navigator. Soon word of the slayings was all over the radio. The names were withheld pending notification of their families.

"Five known drug dealers found dead," boomed through all of the 12" woofers that were tuned into WBLK.

Jovanna heard the announcement on her radio as she was getting ready for bed. She was staying with three young white girls in a rundown two bedroom apartment building on 8th and Ontario. She slept on the sofa. It was old but it was comfortable. She grabbed her purse and ran out the front door.

She ran all the way to Rice's house. She beat on the door over and over again. Then she heard his voice call out, "Who the hell is beating on my door like that this early in the godddamn morning?"

She was relieved to hear his voice but worried now about disturbing him so early in the morning.

Rice snatched the door open ready to confront the intruder. "This better be good, whoever you are." He froze when he saw that it was Jovanna. "Jovanna! Wha-, is something wrong?"

"No! I um, I heard on the radio that somebody, that some young people had gotten killed. I-I came by to-to..." her voice cracked. Her tongue became tied. She was noticeably nervous.

Rice smiled and shifted his weight as he leaned on the door, holding it closed. They both stood there, neither speaking. Neither knowing just what to say. The sound of the toilet flushing filled their silence.

Jovanna jumped as if the sound of the flushing was pulling her down. "Oh, I didn't know you had company." She cried as she turned and started to walk away.

"No wait! She's just. I was going to-, but we, I didn't. Just wait a minute!" Rice went back inside. His voice was barely over a whisper. Seconds later, a young white ho was ushered out by him, fussing up a storm.

"You puttin' me out for her? Hell, she too young to know half the tricks I know. Plus, we didn't even do nuthin' yet, and I need that twenty dollars."

Rice pushed the white girl out and continued to hold the front door open. "Jovanna, please come in."

Jovanna was a little bit heated. But it was funny watching Rice sweat as he dissed the white ho. Jovanna really like the part, *"plus we ain't even did nuthin' yet!"* that was uttered by the white girl. She stepped in and closed the door behind them.

"Baby, is that the kind of shit that you've stooped to since you put me out?"

"Jovanna please. I'm really glad that you came by. I miss the hell out of you. But it also crushed me to sit and watch you chase down tricks."

"I don't chase anybody! They chase me. Except for maybe chasing you."

Rice reached out and grabbed her around her tiny waist and pulled her close. She easily slid upon him.

"I don't kiss customers," she said as Rice leaned in to kiss her.

"Who the hell is a customer," he answered as he snatched her up off of her feet and carried her into his bedroom. He kicked the door shut with his foot.

• • •

By noon the news of the young men's deaths was all over the Falls.

Babybrother packed up most of his clothes, threw the suitcases in the back of his mother's 1988 Buick Century and left town. He was afraid of the idea that this was a revenge killing for stealing the 50 kilos of cocaine and the killing of the two Jamaicans.

Janis woke up her twin sister. "Janet, ain't that the house that Stu hangs out at the house on Elmwood."

Janis jumped up and ran over to the living room television.

Their mother was sitting on the sofa, drinking a large mug of coffee. "That's' what they get. Spreading the devil's candy all over the place. Take a good look, girls. That's the result of boys living in sin. It never pays off. Go to church every Sunday. Save yourself for that man you marry. Live the way that God intended. That's right. Live the way that God intended." The big woman closed her eyes and said a silent prayer.

The names of the deceased men still hadn't been released. The twins went back upstairs to their room.

"Do you think that Stu was in there?"

"Oh, God that would be too good to be true. I mean, I ain't wishing death on nobody, but if he was there and he is dead, then all of this money is ours!"

They'd given him $10,000, and Janet fucked him. Now they had $20,000 and it would have been Janis' turn to be with him. But if... They chose not to talk about it anymore. By tomorrow, they'd know for sure.

Cedric, Cobbs and Scott hit the streets, hitting their normal licks. By 4:00 PM, they were out of dope. People were calling them and stopping them everywhere they went. Rice called and told the fellas that he was sick.

The twins were getting paid on the North side of town while the boys were getting paid on the South. By night fall even the girls were dry. Rice and the fellas cruised up and down the Patch. Several girls would turn tricks and then run to a house on Fairfield.

"Yo, Scott! Who's running that house?"

"Got me Ced, but they about the only niggas in the city with any dope. They's cleanin' up too!"

"Maybe we should go down and talk to the brothers. Maybe they'll sell us a little, 'til we can find some more," suggested Cobbs.

"Yeah and maybe the brothers will just give us some dope so that we can compete with them, when now they practically own the city!" shot Ced.

"I was just offering a suggestion, instead of sitting here doing nothing except complaining."

• • •

At midnight the names of the deceased were announced, Theodore "T-Bone" Bonesworth, Cleveland Simms, Stuart Jones, Charles Black, and Steven Stevens. The report also stated that a large green trunk with lots of cocaine powder residue in it was found in the basement. It was concluded that the deaths were a result of a drug robbery gone bad and that perhaps everyone was killed so that no one would be able to identify the thieves.

Janet and Janis went out to celebrate.

Cedric, Scott and Cobbs tried to figure out who did it and why?

Jennifer, Jill, Sharon, and Tynesha all slept.

Mr. Charlie and the old timers went fishing.

Patsy, Teri and Tara had gone back to Canada.

Stokes was back on the street pushing his shopping cart collecting pop bottles and beer cans.

Chapter Thirty-Six

Geno's wife was sitting in the Niagara Falls Police Station. Her husband had been missing for over a week. Sergeant Steffi was filling out a missing person's report. As they were finishing up, Detective OH, a Korean detective with twenty years service walked up.

"Excuse me, Sergeant. May I have a word with you?"

"Sure, Detective."

Steffi stood up and followed the tiny detective into his office.

"Have a seat, Sergeant. This'll be quick." OH went over to a file cabinet and removed a manila envelope which he handed to Steffi.

Steffi opened it and began reading it. *Black male, age approximately 35-40, height 5'8", bald, light in complexion, weight approximately 160 pounds. Found in green, foot locker, 9:45 AM Wednesday, July 29, 2005.*

"Damn! That sounds like him," said Steffi as he looked over at OH. "Where's the body?"

"Down at County. Do you want me to ask her to go down to ID the body?"

"No, No, I'll handle it. She seems to be such a nice lady too. Damnit!"

Steffi walked back into the lobby and gave Mrs. Johnson the news. She immediately broke down crying.

"Mrs. Johnson, please. Don't cry. We're not even sure that it's him. I'm just asking you to view the body and see if it is him?"

Steffi placed his arm around her shoulders and handed her some tissue to wipe her face.

Mrs. Johnson stood up and slowly walked out to her Mercedes. Steffi opened the door for her. She turned and thanked him. "Thank you Sergeant. Thank you very much, but I've gotta do this on my own. You've been very helpful."

She extended her hand which he covered with his huge mitts. Their hands stayed locked momentarily. Steffi felt the heat rise up his arm. Steffi looked her square in the eyes and said, "Mrs. Johnson, if you need *anything*, anything at all, *please*, call me." And he handed her his card. He was still standing there, staring, as she slowly pulled away.

When Steffi went back inside of the station, Detective OH was standing at this desk. OH's glasses were sitting in his narrow nostrils, instead of the bridge of his nose. Several lines were drawn into his malt-colored brow. Sergeant Steffi knew the look. It was a look he'd seen several times before. Steffi took a deep breath and shuffled toward him.

"Sergeant, have you heard of the massacre on Elmwood Avenue?"

"Uhm yeah. I heard a little about it, several young black men bound and executed. Sounds like a gang thing to me. Sit."

"That's what we thought too. That is, until we found a green trunk in the basement of their house - a trunk identical to the one that Geno Johnson was stuffed in. Quite a coincidence, don't you think?"

"Yes sir!" answered the big goof. His mind wasn't on any damn green trunk. His mind was on the nicely shaped ass of Mrs. Johnson, Geno's wife.

Detective OH saw that he'd failed to gain Sergeant's attention and turned and walked away. When Sergeant Steffi found his way back to his desk, the phone on his desk began to ring. Steffi answered it on the fifth ring. "Hello?"

"961 Fairfield...Drugs...961 Fairfield." Click.

"Hello! Who is this? Hello!" screamed Steffi.

He grabbed a pencil and wrote down the address. *961 Fairfield.* Picking up the phone, he called Detective OH. Minutes later they were sitting on the corner of Highland and Fairfield. Four cars carrying eight cops sat patiently, waiting for the word from OH. Crack hoes kept running in and out getting served within seconds

"Detective, this is *your* show. We're waiting on you," said Detective Wade. Wade was a twelve-year veteran. He'd made his career by busting low to mid level crack dealers.

Sergeant Steffi and three uniformed patrolmen sat in two patrol cars on the left side of the street. Detectives OH and Wade sat on the right with two others.

Inside the house, D-Nice and Stunner were counting money. Their dope was moving better than even they had expected.

"Look, all we need is another six weeks like this, and we can pull up and move out, knowa-I-mean? Huh? Knowa-I–mean?"

"I feel ya, D-Nice, I feel ya. I'm kinda ready to leave this little hick town anyway. Ain't nothing here but a bunch of lames."

"I heard that one. See, up in Atlantic City, we always got something going down...Always...24-7. Know-I-mean? 24-7. Round the clock, know-I-mean?"

OH gave the word. All four cars pulled up in front of the house. The police poured forward surrounding the house. OH knocked on the front door. "Open up! This is Detective OH of the Niagara Falls Police Department!!"

"Oh Fuck, the cops!!!" whispered Stunner while grabbing both of his loaded .44 magnum hand guns.

"What'chu whispering for? They know we in here. Let's give them the kinda special welcoming that Moe and Solo would be proud of, knowa' I mean."

D-Nice put fresh clips in both of his Tek-9's. He locked both weapons, and then blew his nose.

There was another knock at the door, followed by another blast from the bullhorn.

"This is Detective OH. This is your last warning! Come out with your hands up or we'll be forced to come in and get you. We have you surrounded. There is no escape. You have sixty seconds to comply."

Back inside, the two men were passing a blunt of Canada's finest.

"Damn, this shit is good!! I hope that I don't end up wasting a good high," said Stunner as he passed the blunt back to D-Nice.

"Don't even think like that, know I mean? Don't even, know I mean? We gonna be alright. Now is the car ready like we planned?"

"Parked down on Ninth Street."

"Is the money in it?"

"All except today's take."

"Good, and I got today's money right here," said D-Nice as he held up a black duffel bag filled with money and drugs.

Stunner looked at his watch. "Sixty seconds is gone Dee. What'chu wanna do?"

D-Nice hit the last of the blunt and set the roach in a red plastic ashtray. He blew the smoke softly into the air, smiled and said, "Let's go dancing."

Both men ran to the front door. The lights from the patrol cars bounced off of the walls of the house.

"How many do you think are out there?" asked D-Nice.

"I'd guess 8 to 10. Give or take a couple."

"OK, I'll meet you at the car. Knowa' I mean?"

Stunner raised both guns in the air, one in each hand. D-Nice held a tech-9 in each of his arms. Stunner ran out the front door screaming like a mad man. D-Nice opened up with both tech-9's. The police dove to the ground, taking cover as both mad men headed straight at them.

The police started shooting back, but their shots were wide. Stunner opened up with his guns. Two patrolmen fell. Stunner and D-Nice made it to the edge of their lawn, still spraying the cops with bullets. Detective OH was hit in the shoulder. Steffi fell to the ground. He'd gotten hit by one of the barrage of bullets from D-Nice's teks.

One of the remaining patrolmen made it back inside of his patrol car and radioed for help. "This is patrolman Philbeck. We need help *bad*. We are at 961 Fairfield. Four men are down! Repeat. Four officers are down!" As soon as patrolman Philbeck completed his call, he raised his head to see where the two drug dealers were. A bullet from Stunner's .44 magnum removed the top half of his skull.

Bullets were flying all over the place. It was like the fourth of July for a full forty seconds. And then it was over. The two men made it to their parked red Mitsubishi Eclipse. D-Nice jumped behind the wheel and burned rubber, peeling off. They zoomed over to the Robert Moses Parkway. Within seconds, they were gone.

The backup squad cars arrived about the same time that the ambulances did. Four policemen were hit, one fatality. The incident was spread all over the evening news.

The next day Sergeant Steffi was awakened from a somber sleep by a visitor at Memorial Hospital. "Good evening Sergeant, are you alright? I hope that you don't mind my stopping by like this, but I'd heard that you were shot, I-"

Sergeant Steffi wiped his eyes and sat up. "Well no. No I don't mind at all Mrs. Johnson. I don't mind at all."

Chapter Thirty-Seven

Three weeks later...

Cedric, Scott and Cobbs were cruising through the Patch. They had found a new connection, but they were paying significantly more money for a brick than they had ever paid throughout their careers as drug dealers. Even the twins, Janet and Janis had sold out. Ced and his crew had a lock on the city.

"Ced, I wish that we could stumble upon a decent deal on some dope. We could blow up bigger than Nino Brown!" exclaimed the usually mild demeanored Cobbs.

"Yeah, that would be the shit. But I don't have a clue as to where we can find anything better than the 25 that we're paying. Whoever used to supply our area is gone. And that's a fact," stated Ced as he turned up Highland, going over the Highland Bridge.

A man pushing a grocery cart was coming toward the bridge, stopping here and there to pick up empty soda pop, beer bottles and cans.

As the fellows drove closer to the man pushing his cart, Cedric started ribbing on Cobbs. "Hey Cobbs, here comes your father pushing his cart. Why don't you buy your old man a set of spinners for it?"

"Damn, Cobbs, why don't you teach your old man how to dress? Look at him!" joked Scott.

Cobbs looked over at the shabbily dressed man and decided to go along with his buddies' gag. He yelled out, "Yo, Ced! Pull over! Pull over quick!"

Ced hit his brakes and whipped the big red truck over to the curb, startling the older man so badly that he let go of his cart. The cart careened off of the front bumper of the trunk and fell over. Dozens of bottles and cans bounced and rolled all over the sidewalk, filling the curb.

"Oh! Stokes is sorry! Stokes is so, so sorry. Stokes pick up everything. Stokes really am sorry." Stokes began throwing bottles and cans back into his upright cart.

Cobbs hopped out and began to help Stokes clean up his mess. As Cobbs dumped an armload of cans into the tattered black plastic bag that lined the cart, he noticed a duct tape wrapped package, lying in the bottom of the bag.

He reached inside of the bag. A powerful hand gripped around his arm, stopping him from removing the package from the bag.

"That belong to Stokes! Stokes thinks you can go now! Stokes finish."

"Whoa! Hold on brother!" exclaimed Cobbs. "I was just trying to check it out, 'cause if that package is what I think it is, I'll buy it from you?"

Stokes stopped. His hardened face relaxed. "Stokes is listening. How much you gon' pay Stokes for Stokes' package?"

Cobbs stepped back and held his hands up to his chest, palms out. "Now hold on Mr. Stokes." Cobbs always addressed his elders as *Mr.*

"Hold on Mr. Stokes. First me and my partners need to check the package out to make sure it's what I think it is. OK?"

Stokes hesitated, then reached in, pulled the brick of coke out of his cart and handed it to Cobbs saying, "Stokes trust you Cobbs. Treat Stokes right. OK Cobbs? Treat Stokes right."

Cobbs took the brick and nodded at Stokes as he handed the brick to Scott who was sitting on the passenger side of the truck.

"Cobbs gon' treat you right Mr. Stokes. You have my word on that." Cobbs hopped back into the truck.

Scott cut a tiny slit through the duct tape and tasted the white powder that coated the thin blade. "It's good shit, damn good shit!" said Scott as he smacked his lips.

Ced looked out at Stokes. "Give that nigga a hundred dollars and tell him thanks," he ordered.

"I can't do that Ced. I gave my word that I'd lookout. We can't just take the man's stuff. It'll just bring us more bad luck. I don't know about y'all, but I'm getting tired of bad luck. This could be what we've been looking for. This could be that golden opportunity." Cobbs looked at Ced for a response.

Scott looked back at Cobbs. "For once in your otherwise useless life, you made sense. Does your friend have any more? Can we get a lump sum? Like 10 at 10. Now that's a deal for his ass, ten for ten."

"I'll go for that," said Ced. "I'll go for 10 at 10. Go see if he's got anymore."

Cobbs opened the door and called Stokes over. "Hey Mr. Stokes. Would you mind coming over here and joining us, sir? My friends would like to speak to you about this matter of great importance."

Stokes walked over and stood at the open door. "Stokes don't like to ride in trucks. Stokes stand right here."

"OK, OK, suit yourself. What I want to know is, can you get more. Can you get more bricks?"

Stokes could tell that Ced was anxious, so he came straight with it. "Stokes got 44 more bricks. How much you gon' pay Stokes?"

Ced decided to see if the big man knew what he had. "How much do you want big pimpin'?"

Stokes looked over at Cobbs, waiting for an answer.

Cobbs looked at Ced, then at Scott. Finally he blurted out, "10 apiece, ten thousand a brick for all 45 bricks. That's $450,000 Mr. Stokes. You are about to become a very comfortable man."

"Stokes gets four hundred fifty thousand for my packages?"

"Yes sir, Mr. Stokes. Four hundred fifty thousand dollars, but there's only one problem."

"Stokes wants to know what problem?"

"We don't have it all for you today. We'll have to make payments, OK," suggested Cobbs.

"Payments, Stokes don't like payments."

"Look nigga. How do I know that you ain't no cop. You expect me to drop a half a million dollars on you without me even seeing the rest of the product. Nigga please. Scott, toss that nigga's shit and let's bounce." Ced was completely frustrated.

"Hold it! Hold it now!!! Let's get this thing straightened out. Ced, how much do we have? What's the maximum that we can give him?"

Ced looked at the ceiling as he counted up his bank in his head. "I've got about 50 max."

Cobbs turned to Scott and asked, "How much do you have?"

"I've got about 20."

"Good, I've got 30. That's a hundred thousand dollars."

He turned to Stokes. "We've got one hundred thousand dollars now and the rest in payments. Only if you get the rest of the stuff for us today. Today, we have to have the rest, *today."*

Stokes smiled. "Stokes like Cobbs. Cobbs come with Stokes. Stokes give stuff to Cobbs. Cobbs bring Stokes his money." Stokes extended his huge hand. Cobbs shook it.

Cobbs could feel how powerful the huge man was. Cobbs looked at Ced. "Go get the money together. I'll go with Stokes and get the shit."

Two hours later...

Ced, Rice, Scott and Cobbs were checking out each of the bricks of powder. Every one of them was of fish scale quality.

"I wonder where he got this much dope. He doesn't look like he had the money to buy it," stated Rice.

"And he damn sure don't look like he took it," said Scott.

"Who cares? It's ours now. Let's make the most of it," shared Ced.

"Gentlemen, we are on our way. It is now a time of jollification."

"Cobbs, shut the fuck up!"

Chapter Thirty-Eight

Carl had just come home from his job down at the Carborundum Chemical company where he was employed as their Chief Accountant. His wife, Carol had prepared a special meal for him. It was his favorite lasagna, filled with sausage and ground beef, four different cheeses, spinach and her favorite four hour sauce.

Linda, their oldest daughter had just come home from college. This was their winter break. She attended Boston State College, majoring in Political Science for the past three years. Lydia, the youngest of the two siblings had graduated from Niagara Falls High School. *Linda* was class valedictorian. While Lydia was in the bottom half of her class.

Linda was a cheerleader.

Lydia watched all their games from the stands. She hated always being compared to her older sister. Linda always had dozens of boys chasing after her for a date. Lydia had only gone out on prom night. And that was because she'd promised Michael Milkowski a blow job if he took her.

During dinner the doorbell rang. A florist delivered a dozen beautiful red roses. Carl was always thoughtful like that. Always adorning his wife with cards, flowers or jewelry.

After dinner, Carl and Carol drove down to the Falls. This was another of their favorite past times. Holding hands as they watched the sunset over the Falls. The majestic Niagara

Falls. Once they'd even slipped into the bushes for a quickie. Carol kept protesting. "Carl, what if someone sees us?" she'd whisper.

He would always answer her, "Then I'll tell them to find their own. This one's taken." They were reasonably happy.

Back at their house there was a knock at the door. Lydia answered. Two tall handsome college-aged men stood at the door. One was holding a bottle of liquor of some kind. Lydia stood in front of the young men. "Yes?" she asked. She pushed her chest out, hoping that they would notice.

"Is Linda here? She called a few minutes ago and said it was cool to stop by," asked the taller of the two. Both were blondes and Lydia thought that they were just *too* cute.

Before Lydia could answer, Linda came down the stairs dressed in only a bathrobe. She was drying her hair, obviously fresh out of the shower. "Come on up, boys. I've been waiting for you." She turned and tipped the bottom of her robe up at them.

"Not waiting as long as I've been," answered the tallest guy as he ran his fingers through his golden locks and ran up the stairs behind Linda.

Moments later, Lydia could smell the pungent aroma of weed burning. She knew what it was. All of the kids at school smoked it. She'd even tried to a couple of times, but all she did was choke. Lydia ran up stairs and began beating on Linda's locked door. Loud music blasted back at her.

She began to kick the door and scream, "Linda, mom and dad are gonna be furious when they come home. Linda! Linda, you open this door this instant!"

Suddenly the door opened. The tall cute guy was standing there with his shirt off. Curly little locks of blonde hair covered his chest. She wanted to run her fingers across them.

"Hi, I'm Chad," he said. His smile hypnotized her. He stepped away from the door, inviting her in.

Linda was lying on the bed. The other guy was drinking shots off of her stomach. Both of them were laughing uncontrollably. Chad poured liquor into a glass and offered it to Lydia. She refused it.

"Too young, huh? It's good. It's called peppermint schnapps." Chad chugged the drink down, emptying the glass. He poured another shot and offered it again.

Lydia took the glass. *Peppermint schnapps, what can it hurt. It's called peppermint.* She held her nose and poured it down her throat. It burned, but it felt good. And it didn't taste too bad either.

Chad poured her another shot. She downed it too. Then he handed her the blunt. "All of my girls smoke a little cannabis. Don't you want to be like my girls? You're pretty enough to be one."

Chad knew exactly what she wanted to hear. He kept the lines coming, and she took in every one of them. Soon she was lying on the bed next to her drunken sister. Her sister's robe was wide open as the other guy went down on her. Before Lydia realized what was happening Chad was pulling her panties down her long slender legs and off of her feet. Chad kissed every inch of her body, filling her virgin body with desire. Soon both sisters had their legs raised high as the two men punished their vaginas.

The music was loud and everyone was so into what they were doing that they didn't hear their parents when they opened the door to the bedroom. It wasn't until Carl cut on the lights that anybody responded to his presence. Carol screamed and fainted. Carl grabbed her, stopping her from hitting the floor.

Chad, his friend and Linda grabbed their clothes and fled, leaving a naked, drunken Lydia to absorb all of Carl's anger. He cursed Lydia. He called her a whore. He eventually told her to get out of his house. That Linda would never have acted that way, that it was Lydia's fault that everything happened.

Lydia dressed quickly, grabbed her purse and ran out of the house. She walked down to a place on the corner of 56th and Pine- a truck stop called Juniors. She sat at the counter drinking cup after cup of coffee.

By 2:00 AM she decided to go for a walk to get a little air to clean her head. She had only been walking for a few minutes when a black Mercury Marquis pulled up. Two seemingly friendly black men pulled up and offered her a ride.

They introduced themselves as Kenny and Anthony. They even said that they had a big house with five bedrooms, and that she could stay with them until things were cool at home. She shrugged her shoulders and got in, sitting between the two gentlemen. *Why not?* she asked herself, *Why not?*

Chapter Thirty-Nine

Mandy Macombs had just gotten out of the shower. She wrapped her tattered terry cloth robe around her thirty-two year old body and entered into the bedroom. She eyed the clothes that she'd laid out on her bed as she dried herself. Tonight *he* was coming. Whenever he came they would have sex and every time they had sex, he would be awfully generous to her.

She carefully applied lotion to every inch of her body, even between her toes. Her toe nails were freshly painted. She paid extra attention to her feet. She thought back to the last time that he came. She closed her eyes and relived that special way that he had placed her toes into his warm waiting mouth.

She picked up her bottle of scented oil. She couldn't afford perfume. She barely paid the bills that she had. What, with four kids by four different fathers to take care of, it's a wonder that they ate.

She applied a little on the insides of her thighs, the crook of her arms, her wrist and behind each ear. "Eat it Raw", that's what the oil was called. He said that he liked how it smelled on her, and tonight she aimed to please.

She put on her black lace panties with the matching bra. She dabbed a little Ban deodorant on and picked up her pride and joy, a red after five dress by Gloria Vanderbilt. She loved that dress. She loved the way it hugged her hips and waist, making her appear at least ten pounds lighter. She loved the way that it held her breasts up and out. She was built rather nice for a woman her age with four kids. She decided against panty hose. He liked to run his hands up and under her dress. Panty hose were just a nuisance for times like that.

She applied mascara, eye liner and a dark cherry lipstick that blended perfectly with her cocoa brown complexion. She unwrapped the silk scarf that was tied about her head. She combed and patted her just permed hair. She owed her sister, Tamika fifteen dollars for buying and applying her perm.

She slipped into her size 7½ red pumps and ran to peek out of the living room window. The street was dark except fore the one working street light about five houses down. Other than that the street was bare. She picked up Camille's long black satin top coat. She'd borrowed it from her neighbor just for tonight.

Toot-Toot!

A car horn honked. Her heart raced. She ran back to the window, but it wasn't him. Tracy, the young girl across the street ran out and jumped into a Cadillac Eldorado with three young men inside. She watched until they pulled off, headed to who knows where.

She went to the kitchen and prepared a bottle of milk for Thomas Jr. She couldn't wait until he was off of that damn bottle. Hell, milk was $2.99 a gallon. She was teaching him to say "cup". As soon as he got that word down pat, the bottle was gone. She set the bottle in a pot and added some water to it. Then set the pot on the stove.

Toot-Toot!

Another car horn. Again she went to the window. Again she was disappointed.

An hour went by, then another. He said that he'd be there at nine. Now it was 11:15 PM. She went next door to Camille's house to use her phone. He didn't like to be called. He was a married man, but tonight was going to be special. He said so. He promised.

Mandy called. He said that he'd gotten tied up with something and that he'd be there in a few minutes. She hung up.

Camille told her how pretty she looked, but also warned her not to mess up her $200 coat. Mandy assured her that she would replace the coat if it were to get damaged in any way.

When Mandy returned home, her oldest son, Saheeb was warming the bottle on the stove while holding Thomas Jr.

"I thought that you had a date, mama?"

"I do Saheeb, but we're running a little late. We'll be leaving shortly."

"Mama, I need two dollars to go on a field trip Monday. I missed the last field trip 'cause we ain't have no money. Can I go this time mama? Please mama? I've been good. All of us have been good."

Saheeb spoke the truth. All four of her boys had been wonderful children. No trouble in school. Good grades and all. They kept their rooms clean and did the dishes every day. She ran her fingers through his frizzy hair. His cornrows needed to be redone. She'd do them in the morning.

"Sure, sure you can go." She said.

"Promise mom? You promise I can go?"

"I said yeah! I promise you can go."

A smile three feet wide zoomed across his face. He hopped up still holding his brother and took the bottle out of the pot. He shook the bottle up and tested it on his wrist. Perfect. All he wanted to do was to take a little chill off of it. He'd learned that cold milk would sometimes wake his brother fully, but if he just took the chill off of it, little Thomas Jr. would fall fast asleep, and usually sleep the rest of the night.

Toot-Toot.

Another car horn. She ran to the window and peeked out. Her heart pounded with joy as she looked out at the big black Mercedes Benz 500.

"Baby, mama's gone! Take care of everything and I'll see you guys in the morning. Okay?"

"Okay mama!"

Out the door she ran. She ran all the way up to the side of the car and swung open the passenger door. A tall sexily dressed Hispanic girl stepped out. A trail of mixed perfume, alcohol and weed came out with her. Mandy slid in next to her date. The tall woman slid in next to *her* and pulled the door shut. The big black sedan pulled off.

Many looked at her date, then leaned over and kissed him on the cheek. "Hi baby! What's up?" she asked.

He smiled and wet his lips. "Why *you* are what's up, my sweet. As you always are."

Mandy blushed. He always made her feel real special. She loved it when he called her his sweets.

They rode for awhile, heading out of Center Court toward the bars and the Patch. Mandy knew the routine. They'd go to one of the Highland Avenue bars for a few drinks where he could show everyone in the club how much in control he was by grabbing her ass and kissing her breasts. And the time when he fingered her while they sat with a table full of people.

Then, they'd go to a motel, usually the Pelican where he would fuck her brains out. They'd sleep and he'd drop her off with a couple of hundred dollars for her troubles.

But now...*this woman... What part did she play in the routine?* Mandy wanted to know but was afraid to ask.

They pulled up to 3 Brothers Bar, the nicest, largest bar in the hood. He parked and helped them out of the car. He took one on each arm and escorted them into the club. They were seated at their usual seats. He ordered their usual drinks. He cavorted with both women, touching both of their breasts and grabbing both of their behinds, until the bar closed. They were all feeling pretty good.

Once they were loaded back into the car, Mandy asked, "What are we going to do with her?" She pointed at the Hispanic chic while leaning on his big broad shoulders, shoulders that seemed even larger then normal.

He laughed aloud. "Everything, my sweets. We are going to do absolutely everything with her. That's why I told you that tonight was going to be special. She's your surprise."

Mandy froze. *He wants to fuck us both? Hell naw!* she thought. *Hell naw! He's mine. He's my way out of my financial problems.*

Her head began to sway from the alcohol. The Hispanic lady lit up a blunt and inhaled. A hand appeared on Mandy's thigh, inching slowly upward. The Hispanic girl leaned over and slowly began to blow the smoke into Mandy's face. Mandy opened her mouth and began to suck in the smoke that the Hispanic girl was blowing.

Closer and closer, the Hispanic woman came closer to Mandy's open mouth. Then their lips touched. Mandy felt the soft, sweet wet tip of the girl's tongue ease into her mouth. The hand on her thigh had pushed the black lace panties aside and was slowly stroking her clit. That's when she noticed that the hand on her thigh was not his, it was hers!

"No! Stop! Stop the fucking car!" she demanded.

The car pulled over to the curb and stopped. Mandy continued to scream. "Stop it. Stop it goddamnit! I don't get down like that! I don't even know this bitch's name, but I'm supposed to fuck her!"

"Her fucking name is Gabrielle!" he screamed. "Now can we continue on without you having a piss fit?"

"A piss fit? Is that what you call it? A piss fit. Well what do you call this?" Mandy hauled off and punched Gabrielle in the nose as hard as she could with her left hand. Blood shot out all over Camille's black coat.

The smell of something burning alarmed all of them. Gabrielle held her nose catching a handful of blood.

"Something's burning in my car. Get out! Both of you whores get out of my car!" He ordered them both out.

Gabrielle opened the door and both girls jumped out. Mandy looked down and saw several yellow burning embers on the bottom of Camille's coat.

He checked the floor and seats of his car. "Fucking whores," was all the girls heard before he climbed back into his car and sped off. Both girls were left behind.

Gabrielle stepped out into the street and hailed a passing taxi. Mandy had no money, so she began to walk. She walked a dozen blocks heading home. She thought, *How am I going to pay for Camille's coat? How am I going to pay Tamika for doing my hair? And what about my promise to Saheeb?*

Tears began to run down her face. She couldn't go home, not now. She had to get some money. She continued to walk, getting more and more sober with each step.

She walked back down to Highland, hoping that her date was still out riding around. There was still enough time. She admitted that she'd committed the ultimate sin. She'd fallen for her trick. She reacted the way she did out of jealousy, plain and simple.

She walked on down to the Patch. Several groups of girls paraded around, displaying their wares, tight skirts, extremely short pants, and bare breasts, whatever it took. Mandy took a deep breath and removed her coat. She was definitely the most expensive looking piece of ass on the block. She hadn't taken ten good steps before a white BMW with two men in it approached her, *Window Shopping.*

"Hey baby! What's up?"

She looked at both men. Mid forty's, both a tad overweight. She kept walking.

"Look mama! Our money is just as good as the rest. See!" The passenger held out a fist full of twenty's.

Mandy stopped. "How much of that can a girl get?" she asked.

"As much as a fine assed bitch like you can want. Are you down?"

Mandy took another deep breath. *I promised I promised,* she thought. She held the black coat up in the air. She wiped a new tear from her eye with it, then dropped it on the ground and got inside the car.

Conclusion

Tara was just finishing her last set at the Sundowner Strip Club when a waiter called her over to a darkened booth. Cautiously she walked over to it. "Stokes? Is that you Stokes?"

"Hello my beautiful friend. How are you and your beautiful friends Patsy and Teri?"

"They're fine, but how are you? What brings you over?"

"Stokes came to give this to his friends."

Stokes handed her a brown paper bag. She grabbed it and opened it. Her eyes widened, her mouth dropped. Then a wide smile crossed her face.

"I don't understand. What's this for?" she asked.

Stokes stood up. "It's for Stokes' friends. Stokes wants to help his friends. You are the only friends Stokes has."

Suddenly three young white American drunks came by. They stopped and began harassing Tara. One of them grabbed her arm and spun her around to face him. He spun her so hard that the strap on her top snapped, exposing her breast.

Stokes grabbed the young man in his powerful hands and tossed him across the room. The other two men charged him. Stokes swung and hit one of them in the stomach, stopping him in his tracks. The third stopped, turned and ran.

Stokes took off his jacket and covered Tara with it. She kissed Stokes on his forehead. He blushed.

"Stokes got to go now. But Stokes will be back. Stokes promise. Stokes miss you. Stokes miss you a lot."

Stokes started to walk away. He'd only taken a few steps away from Tara when he stopped and looked back at her. Tears filled his eyes. And then he was gone.

Tara took the bag home and counted it. $25,000 American. She quickly called Patsy, Teri, Summer, and Kimberly and told them about Stokes' visit.

Janet and Janis were busy buying up material and making clothes. Getting everything ready for the magic show in Las Vegas. Money was plentiful now that they didn't have to pay Stu. They had everything that they'd needed to launch their clothing line, *Strawberry Patch Clothing.*

Ashley and Amber had entered the first step center for alcohol and drugs. Lisa landed a job at McDonalds. Lisa and her mom Laura were at least talking to each other again. Old Karen got married to the guy that worked at the plant.

D-Nice and the Stunner made it back to Atlantic City where they sold all of their dope and bought a club, *The Reason Why.* Strippers and alcohol had replaced the hits of crack.

An anonymous person deposited $25,000 in the commissary accounts of Moe and Solo. Both of their families also received anonymous gifts of $100,000 each.

Sergeant Steffi was dating the Johnson widow. Word on the street was that he was sprung wide open. That mature black pussy had blown his mind.

Mr. Charlie was trying his hand at writing books. The girls were pretty much gone. Sharon had contracted AIDS. Jennifer was paralyzed from the waist down. She'd gotten caught with her fingers in a trick's pants pockets and he'd beaten her unconscious. She never regained the use of her legs. Tynesha was pregnant and living with her fiancé. They both still attended the meetings at A.A. and N.A. Jill was in jail for soliciting for the purpose of prostitution.

Strawberry was gone. No one knew where. One day she just up and disappeared again. Sometimes it's best that things ended up the way they did.

Me, Chris, Well me and Nae Nae we're alright. I found out how much I need and love her. I've even forgiven her for what she did to Strawberry. Hell, she was only trying to protect her family and keep her man.

Sheka, Amanda, Detroit, Pittsburgh and New York were all back up in county jail. They were busted passing counterfeit hundred dollar bills.

Jovanna was still with Rice. They'd moved into a nice house out in LaSalle, close to where I live. Word had it that she was pregnant.

The limo business is better than ever. I still send Mrs. Johnson her money each month. I feel that I owe it to Geno, even though he had never signed any legal documents proving his partnership. He never made any arrangements in case of death either.

Niagara Falls, New York is home to me. Every inch of it. From Devoe to LaSalle, from Unity park to Center Court, from Falls Street to Park Place. From the melting pot of people staying in the hotels and casinos, to the millions of people that frequent the majestic Falls.

Whether it be the lawmaking people at City Hall or the law *breaking* people down at the Strawberry Patch, Niagara Falls is the place to be. And if you're ever in town, do a little *Window Shopping*. You might end up with a little more than you expected.

Dedications

This book is deedicated to all of my children. Latitia (Shana), Charles (Lil Hood), Tamera', Markeesha (Keewee), Christopher (Kris), Jacqueline (JJ), Cameron (Cam) and Marrissa (Rissa). And to their baby brother, Brandon.

To my father Major Threat, grandma etta Shelton, brothers ralph Eugene, Curtis James, Darrell leon and Major Lynn. My only sister Etta Sutton. And to all of my nieces, nephews, aunts, uncles and to the hundreds of cousins that I have.

Be watching for the Window Shopper II !!!!

Fan Mail

contact

Charles Threat

mr_charlie716@yahoo.com

or at

Amiaya Entertainment, LLC
P.O. Box 1275
New York, NY 10159

Flower's Bed
The Most Controversial Book Of This Era
Written By
Antoine "Inch" Thomas
Suspenseful...Fastpaced...Richly Textured
Published By Amiaya Entertainment

From the Underground Bestseller "Flower's Bed"
Author Antoine "Inch" Thomas delivers you
NO REGRETS
It's Time To Get It Popping
"Gritty....Realistic Conflicts....Intensely Eerie"
Published by Amiaya Entertainment

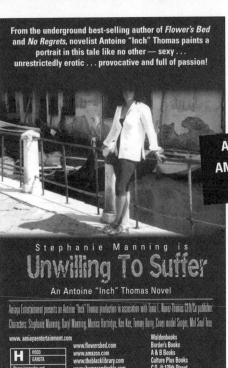

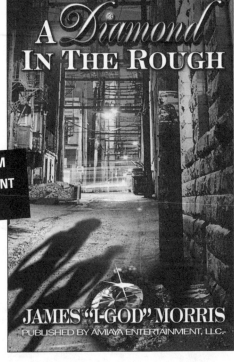

AVAILABLE NOW FROM
AMIAYA ENTERTAINMENT
ISBN# 0-9745075-3-9

AVAILABLE NOW FROM
AMIAYA ENTERTAINMENT
ISBN# 0-9745075-7-1

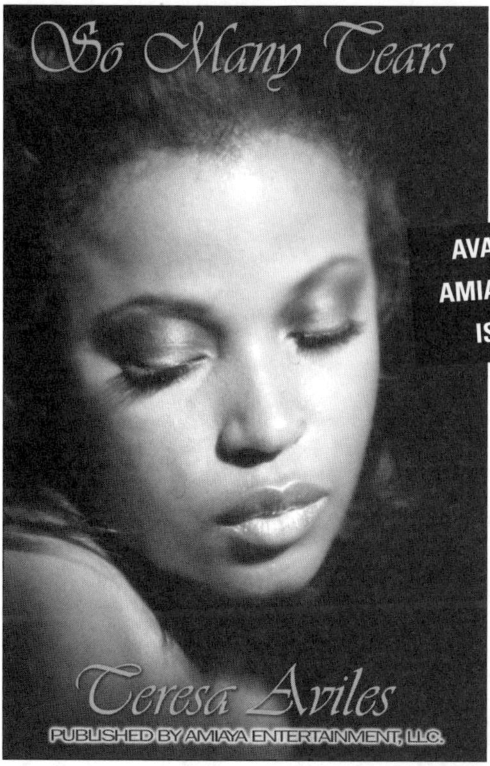
So Many Tears
Teresa Aviles
PUBLISHED BY AMIAYA ENTERTAINMENT, LLC.

HOE-ZETTA
VINCENT WARREN BRINGS YOU ANOTHER "HOT" NOVEL FROM AMIAYA ENTERTAINMENT
VINCENT "V.I." WARREN
PUBLISHED BY AMIAYA ENTERTAINMENT, LLC.

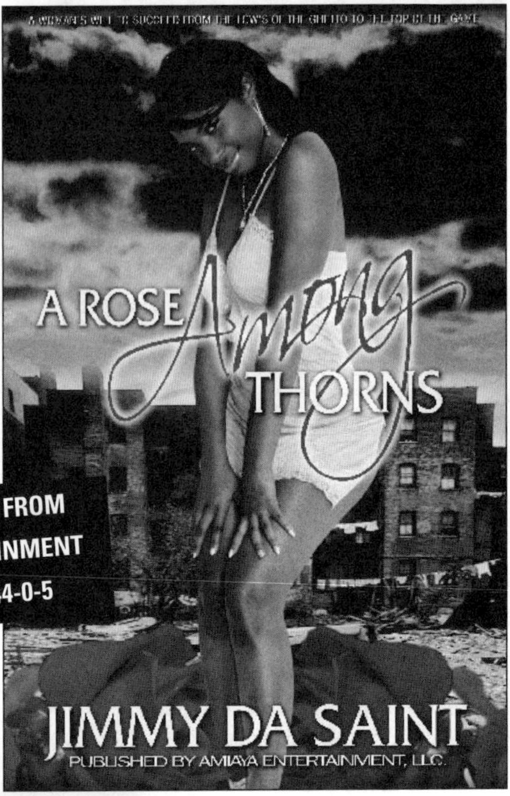
A ROSE
Among
THORNS
JIMMY DA SAINT
PUBLISHED BY AMIAYA ENTERTAINMENT, LLC.

"THEY DONT THUG NI#&AS OUT LIKE WE DO"
THAT
GANGSTA
SH!T
VOL. II
Featuring Antoine "INCH" Thomas
HERE COMES THE PAIN
PUBLISHED BY AMIAYA ENTERTAINMENT, LLC.

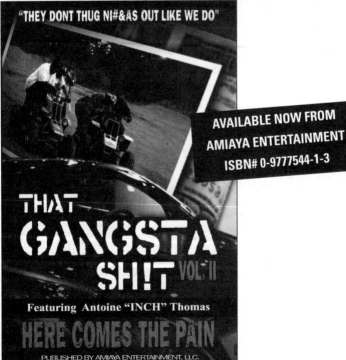

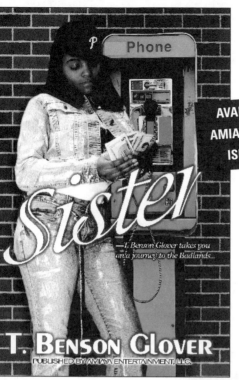

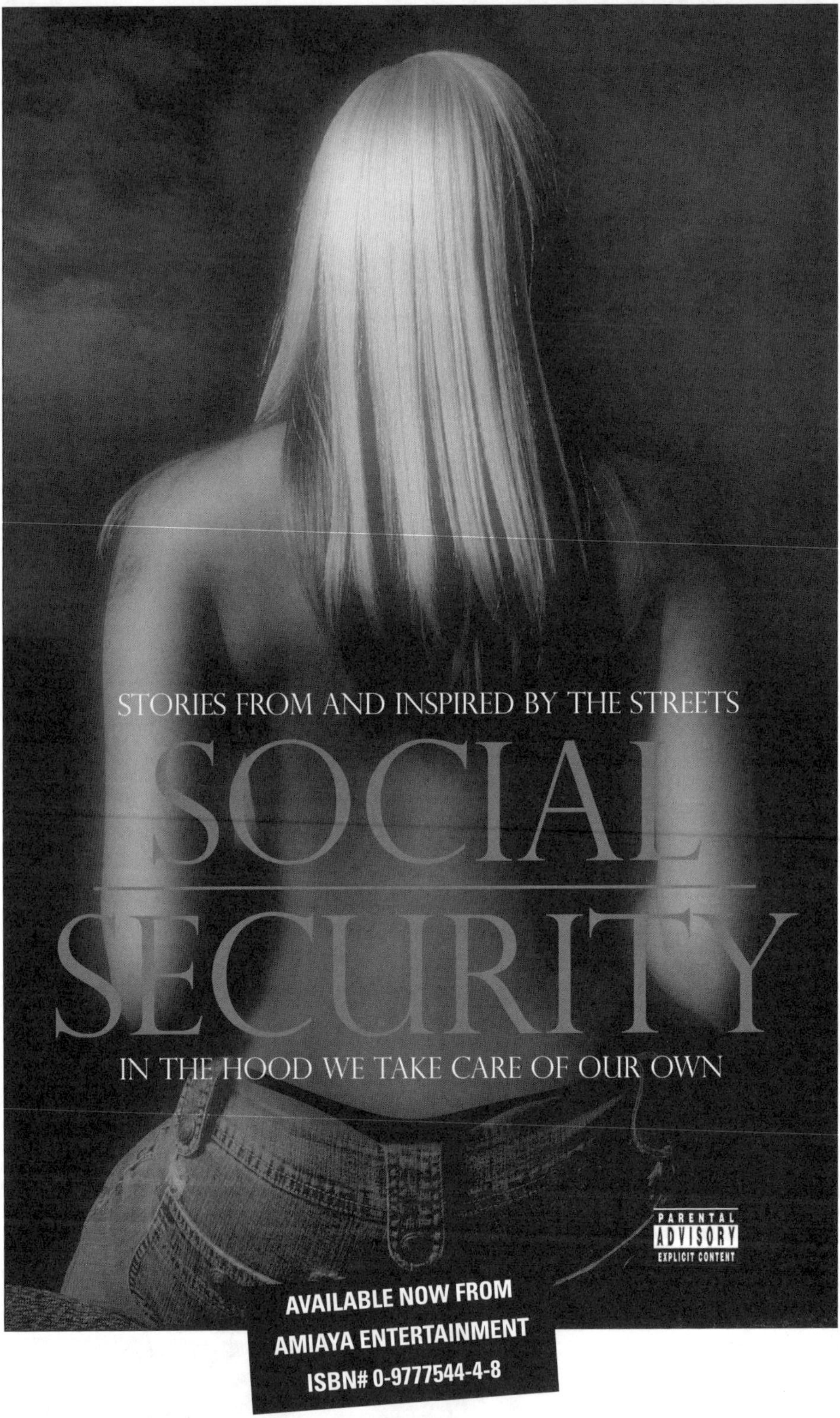
STORIES FROM AND INSPIRED BY THE STREETS
SOCIAL SECURITY
IN THE HOOD WE TAKE CARE OF OUR OWN
PARENTAL ADVISORY EXPLICIT CONTENT
AVAILABLE NOW FROM
AMIAYA ENTERTAINMENT
ISBN# 0-9777544-4-8

Here TODAY
GONE Tomorrow
J.MARCELLE
AVAILABLE SUMMER 2007
AMIAYA ENTERTAINMENT
ISBN# 978-0-9777544-5-6

Flower's Bed
THE SEQUEL
Black Roses
Written By
Antoine "Inch" Thomas
PUBLISHED BY AMIAYA ENTERTAINMENT, LLC.

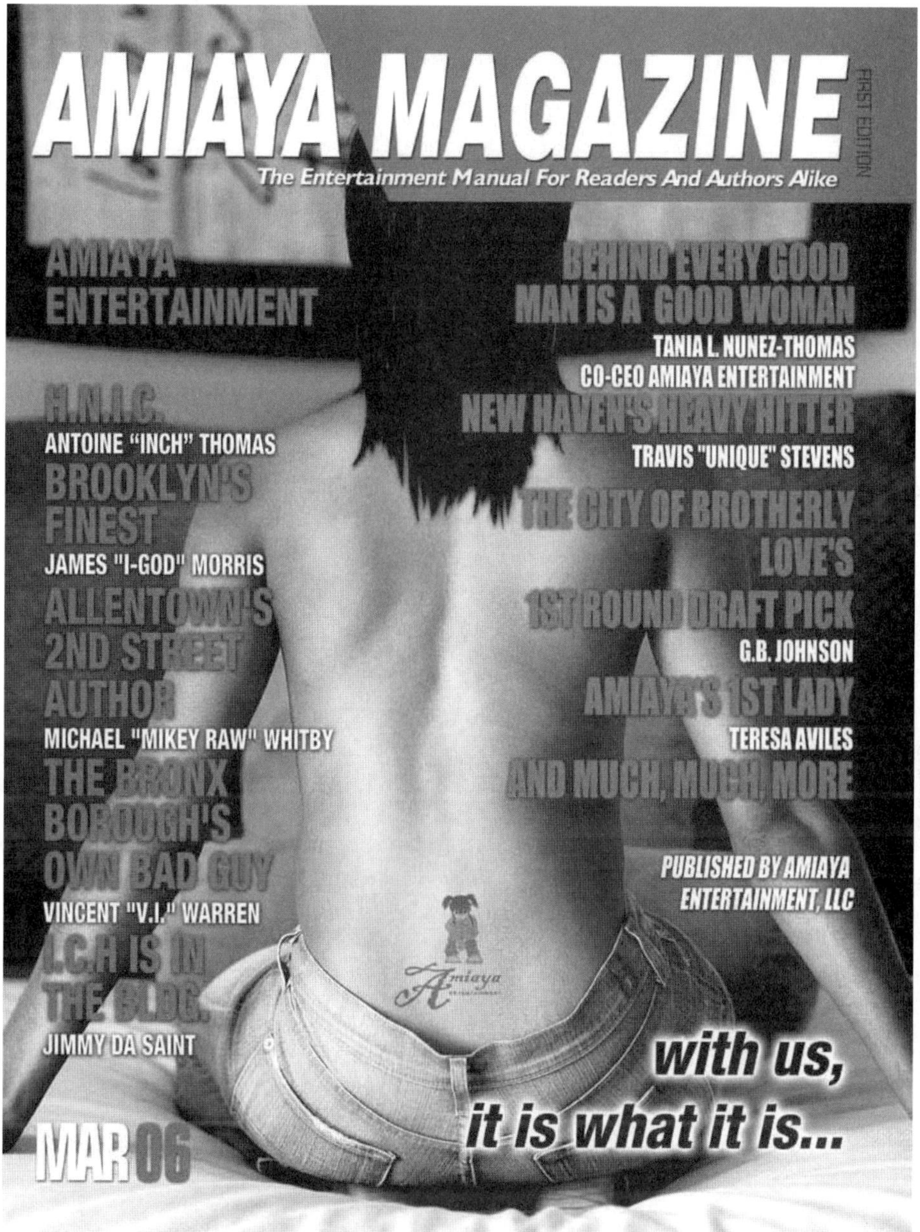
AMIAYA MAGAZINE
FIRST EDITION
The Entertainment Manual For Readers And Authors Alike
AMIAYA ENTERTAINMENT
BEHIND EVERY GOOD MAN IS A GOOD WOMAN
TANIA L. NUNEZ-THOMAS
CO-CEO AMIAYA ENTERTAINMENT
H.N.I.C.
ANTOINE "INCH" THOMAS
NEW HAVEN'S HEAVY HITTER
TRAVIS "UNIQUE" STEVENS
BROOKLYN'S FINEST
JAMES "I-GOD" MORRIS
THE CITY OF BROTHERLY LOVE'S
1ST ROUND DRAFT PICK
G.B. JOHNSON
ALLENTOWN'S 2ND STREET AUTHOR
MICHAEL "MIKEY RAW" WHITBY
AMIAYA'S 1ST LADY
TERESA AVILES
AND MUCH, MUCH MORE
THE BRONX BOROUGH'S OWN BAD GUY
VINCENT "V.I." WARREN
PUBLISHED BY AMIAYA ENTERTAINMENT, LLC
I.C.H IS IN THE BLDG.
JIMMY DA SAINT
Amiaya
with us,
it is what it is...
MAR 06

Window Shopper
ORDER FORM

		Number of Copies
Window Shopper	ISBN# 978-0-9777544-6-4	$15.00/Copy___
Flower's Bed the Sequel	ISBN# 978-0-9777544-8-0	$15.00/Copy___
Street Karma	ISBN# 978-0-9777544-7-2	$15.00/Copy___
Here Today Gone Tomorrow	ISBN# 978-0-9777544-5-6	$15.00/Copy___
Social Security	ISBN# 0-9777544-4-8	$15.00/Copy___
Sister	ISBN# 0-9777544-3-X	$15.00/Copy___
A Rose Among Thorns	ISBN# 0-9777544-0-5	$15.00/Copy___
That Gangsta Sh!t Vol. II	ISBN# 0-9777544-1-3	$15.00/Copy___
So Many Tears	ISBN# 0-9745075-9-8	$15.00/Copy___
Hoe-Zetta	ISBN# 0-9745075-8-X	$15.00/Copy___
All or Nothing	ISBN# 0-9745075-7-1	$15.00/Copy___
Against The Gain	ISBN# 0-9745075-6-3	$15.00/Copy___
I Ain't Mad At Ya	ISBN# 0-9745075-5-5	$15.00/Copy___
A Diamond In The Rough	ISBN# 0-9745075-4-7	$15.00/Copy___
Flower's Bed	ISBN# 0-9745075-0-4	$15.00/Copy___
That Gangsta Sh!t	ISBN# 0-9745075-3-9	$15.00/Copy___
No Regrets	ISBN# 0-9745075-1-2	$15.00/Copy___
Unwilling To Suffer	ISBN# 0-9745075-2-0	$15.00/Copy___

PRIORITY POSTAGE (4-6 DAYS US MAIL): Add $4.95

Accepted form of Payments: Institutional Checks or Money Orders

(All Postal rates are subject to change.)

Please check with your local Post Office for change of rate and schedules.

Please Provide Us With Your Mailing Information:

lling Address____________________	Shipping Address
ame:____________________	Name:____________________
ddress:____________________	Address:____________________
ite/Apartment#:____________________	Suite/Apartment#:____________________
ty:____________________	City:____________________
o Code:____________________	Zip Code:____________________

(Federal & State Prisoners, Please include your Inmate Registration Number)

Send Checks or Money Orders to:
AMIAYA ENTERTAINMENT
P.O.BOX 1275
NEW YORK, NY 10159

1 646-331-3258

MelSoulTree
Soul Quest Records
International Vocalist
MelSoulTree
FEATURING
IN STORES NOW!!
www.MelSoulTree.com

Melissa Thomas, born and raised in the New York City Borough of the Bronx is both beautiful and talented! **MEL-SOUL-TREE** (Melissa Rooted In Soul), a sensational R&B soul singer (with a strong background in Gospel music) is signed to the international **Soul Quest Record Label**. This vocalist has been described as having "an **AMAZING** voice that is **EMOTIONALLY CHARGED** to deliver the goods through her **INCREDIBLE** vocal range."

MelSoulTree can sing!! (Log on to www.Soundclick.com/MelSoulTree to hear music excerpts and view her video "Rain" from her self-titled debut **CD**). **MelSoulTree** has performed worldwide. She has established musical ties in France, Germany, Switzerland, Argentina, Uruguay, Chile, Canada and throughout the U.S.

LIVE PERFORMANCES?

MelSoulTree's love for performing in front of live audiences has earned her a loyal fan base. This extraordinary artist is blessed, not only as a soloist, but has proven that she can sing with the best of them. **MelSoulTree's** rich vocals are a mixture of **R&B, Hip Hop, Gospel and Jazz** styles. This songbird has been blessed with the gift of song. "Everyone speaks the same language when it comes to music, and every time I perform on stage, I realize how blessed I am."

PERFORMANCE HISTORY

MelSoulTree has worked with music legends such as: **Sheila Jordan, Ron Carter, The Duke Ellington Orchestra, The Princeton Jazz Orchestra & Ensemble, Smokey Robinson, Mickey Stevenson, Grand Master Flash** and the **Glory Gospel Singers** to name a few. This sensational vocalist has also recorded for the **Select, Wild Pitch, Audio Quest, Giant/Warner, Lo Key** and **2 Positive** record labels. She tours internationally both as a soloist and as a member of the legendary **Crystals (a group made popular in the 1960's by Phil Spector's "Wall of Sound")**. **MelSoulTree** is known affectionately as the "Kid" or "Baby" by music legends on the veteran circuit. "Working with the **Crystals** has afforded me priceless experience, both on stage and in the wings being 'schooled' by other legendary acts while on these tours." According to **MelSoulTree**, "performing and studying the live shows of veteran acts is the most effective way to learn to engage an audience and keep my performance chops on point at the same time."

MUSICAL INFLUENCES

Minnie Riperton, Phyllis Hyman, Stevie Wonder, Marvin Gaye, Chaka Khan, Natalie Cole, Rachelle Farrell, CeeCee Winans, Ella Fitzgerald, Whitney Houston, Alicia Keys, Mariah Carey, Yolanda Adams and many others... "A lot can be learned from new school and old school artists... good music is good music! I want to be remembered for bringing people **GREAT** music and entertainment!!

Support the Soul Quest Records **MelSoulTree Project** by ordering your CD TODAY!

MelSoulTree's "Mel-Soul-Tree" **CD ALBUM**/ISBN# 8-3710109095-7 ***$16.98***/Per CD______

10 Songs + 2 Remixes

*** ***SPECIAL "MAIL ORDER" PROMOTION*** ***

FREE "FIRST CLASS" SHIPPING **ANYWHERE** IN THE UNITED STATES.

FREE Autographed POSTER when you buy **2 or MORE** MelSoulTree CD Albums.

Hurry! This FREE Poster Promotion is available while supplies last!!!

Please allow 7 Days for delivery. Accepted forms of payment: Checks or Money Orders.

CREDIT CARD ORDERS can be placed via www.CDBaby.com/MelSoulTree2

OR

Call CD Baby at: **1 (800) Buy-My-CD**

NOTE: Credit Card Orders will be charged $16.98 + S&H. Credit Card orders are NOT eligible for the FREE poster offer.

Please provide us with your BILLING & SHIPPING information:

BILLING ADDRESS

Name:______________________________

Address:______________________________

Suite/Apt.:______________________________

City: ______________ State: ______________ Zip Code: __________

SHIPPING ADDRESS

Name:______________________________

Address:______________________________

Suite/Apt.:______________________________

City: ______________ State: ______________ Zip Code: __________

If you are ordering 2 or MORE CD's... Please list the name(s) that should be signed on the FREE autographed poster. ______________

Send Checks or Money Orders along with this form to:

Soul Quest Records
244 Fifth Avenue, Suite K210
New York, NY 10001-7604
www.MelSoulTree.com

We thank you in advance for your support of the Soul Quest Records MelSoulTree Project. www.MelSoulTree.com